Be Quick,
Be Clever,
Be Wild!

— Gandersnitch

The
COMPLETELY
INAPPROPRIATE
TALES of
GANDERSNITCH
the GOBLIN

The COMPLETELY INAPPROPRIATE INAPPROPRIATE TALES of GANDERSNITCH the GOBLIN

by Robert A. Turk

Robert A Turk

6/6/15

Goblin Road
Publishing Co.

For Strange Company

Especially Azog
(but only the good parts)

Queens
Village

The Catoctin Mts

Boggy Bottoms

The Dismal Forest

The Aerie

The Cliffs of Calamity

GOBLONIA

A MAP OF
THE GOBLIN REALMS

Illustrated by The Accidental Cartographer, M. Hindman
as construed by Gangersnitch the Goblin

Contents

Come my pretty,
Come my child,
Come to our Gob-a-lin ball.
Come dance with dark mischievous things,
And feast in our bloody hall.

Come my pretty,
Come my child,
Come so far away.
But be you quick, and clever, and wild,
Or here, forever, you'll stay.

—a traditional Goblin invitation

The Prologue

A WOMAN'S SOFT VOICE called to me through the foggy stillness of the twilight woods. "Gandersnitch the Goblin. Do mine eyes see true? Can it really be you?"

Her intonation was as chill as the autumn air that gnawed at the tips of my ears and my nose, but my first instinct was still excitement, as this was a voice that hinted at high breeding and a poetic affectation. Though my back was to her, I imagined I could see the glint of starlight in her jewels, smell the musk of her fine perfume over the cloying rot of damp dead leaves, and taste the sweetness of her graceful lips dripping perhaps with honey and dew. Maybe my night was looking up after all, even though she had caught me in the unseemly act of emptying my bladder amongst a tangle of briars.

"After years of circling, our paths have finally crossed this very night. How terribly unfortunate for us both. I had been entertaining the thought of other amusements for this October evening." I now realized that I knew this voice, and all my hopes of a sensual romp amongst slumming nobility were summarily dashed into the dirt. This was the voice of the Queen of Faerie, the dread Titania.

I had heard no footsteps crunching through the fallen leaves. There was no jingle of harness or whinny of a horse. One moment I had been alone, tending to my private affairs, and the next I had a spear point poking me sharply in the back. I had no choice but to continue with my ablutions, as this might be my final act of defiance against a cruel and delusional regime. It was fortunate, perhaps, that I had already been in the middle of them, and thus not prompted to ruin my trousers when taken so rudely by surprise. It would not do to die in a puddle of my own making, after all.

"Poor banished Gandersnitch," the Queen mused in annoyance as I stood there with my back to her still. "How far you have fallen. Not even a pot... as they would say. I had almost given up the fancy that we would ever apprehend you. I do hope that you will forgive me, but I would be thought the fool if I did not immediately place you under arrest."

Had she caught me fairly, the Queen of Faerie? It is hard to say for certain. For so long I had skirted through the fringes of both worlds. An outlaw and a fugitive, banished from my own lands, unwelcome in hers, and just managing to get by in yours. The mortal realms that is, this place you call home. Midgard, Earth, Gaia, New Jersey—whatever title you prefer. This is where she had finally found me. Pissing in the woods.

I had been running and hiding for almost three hundred years and frankly I was tired. Maybe in a sense I had simply given up, dropped my guard, and let myself get caught. The seelie sorts had not been actively hunting me all that time, as I simply wasn't worth the trouble to them. But the goblin chieftains had, and my past crimes made it difficult to find hospitality among any who were connected to the faerie courts.

It was an understandable, if unfortunate, position that I existed in. I was rotten and dangerous, a truly unrepentant cad. And I had been accused on occasion of being slightly depraved. I had left in my wake a string of broken hearts, bloody corpses, pilfered fortunes, and one night stands. Maybe it was time to finally face the music with a bow. I stowed my baggage and buttoned up my fly before turning around at last with a wry and wicked smile.

The Queen Titania had many forms, and I knew she would always assume the one most suitable to those who witnessed her. What I saw was a thirty something elvish lass, as I would never imagine a goblin woman as the queenly sort. She was thin and graceful with tender knowing eyes and honey colored hair pulled up into a twist. Her skin was pale, her breeches tight, and her chest flattened beneath the fine leather doublet that she wore. A simple circlet of silver graced her brow, and a shining silver sword hung at her hip. She was a warrior to my eyes, a captain of field and forest instead of a dainty figurehead on a silken tuffet. One false move and I knew my head would be at her feet with my shoulders to follow soon after.

I held up my hands to show that I was not resisting, and then reached slowly down to remove my scissors and wand and toss them to the ground beside me. I did not kneel, nor did I bow or grovel. I was not one to face my fortunes like a cur begging for her favor and mercy.

Her two guards and sometimes lovers, rivals through the seasons for her hand and her bed, lowered their spears and stepped forward to secure my weaponry. The wand gave them a bit of trouble, being as it was cold iron forged in the shape of a simple well-worn stick. I had built up a resistance to its bite over the years, aided by my natural hobgoblin affinity for human implements, but the gloves I wore were not just to keep my hands warm. Eventually, the Duke of Summer managed to wrap it up in leaves and carry it a safe distance away from his lady.

She stood there motionless, simply watching me with a thin smirk on her lips, and neither coldness nor warmth in her bright green eyes. That has always been my problem with royalty, their distant aloofness. They find it so hard to relate to the common folk, and for the alien minds of faeries, this is doubly so.

✖ ✖ ✖ ✖

But I am not a faerie, you see. There might be some confusion on that point, depending on which human scholar you choose to believe. If my estimation counts for anything, then I say that it doesn't really matter how you break it all down in the end. The fact exists that there are secret paths and hidden ways, and those, like myself, who reside in such places are other than human.

The early English called my kind a "hobgoblin", which is a bit different than your common Germanic goblin. I am copper skinned, instead of green, and fond of whiskey, women, and fine clothes. On the whole my sort is not violent, just mischievous, and we often live well in the houses of men. I was the exception to that rule. In a sense, I still am.

Even now I claim no house as my own and travel where I will, seeking my fortune and my fame once more. Most nights will find me as this one does, sitting alone in the shadowy corner of an aged pub, off the beaten path, and sipping at my whiskey through a straw. Perhaps that is not the most acceptable way to imbibe this vice of mine, but it sure beats getting my nose all sticky in the glass.

Tonight, as I write these words, a bottle of Jameson is close at hand. It is good for drowning the sorrows and conjuring forth the shades of the past without fear. I am always amused by the fact that it seems green in the bottle, and yet pours a light amber in the glass. The scent of old charred wood wafting from the whiskey is refreshing. The friendly sandpapery burn at the back of the throat as each sip warms my blood is welcome. The slight impression of wet and moldy cardboard... Well, that is more of an acquired taste. But now back to the memories at hand.

✖ ✖ ✖ ✖

"You have never done me any personal harm, barber. But I must endeavor to keep the peace as well as I am able. If I turn you over to those who seek you, it will mean a rather messy end, won't it?" The Queen was stalling, dragging me along with her words, and I knew not why.

I gave the slightest of nods to her question but said nothing. I had nothing to say. What excuses could I have offerd to this fair and noble being? What interest would she have had in my tale? I was a gnat, a nuisance. Nothing more in her eyes than a lowly hob.

And then, with a cruel twist of her lips, her trap snapped shut. "Then this is my gift to you, goblin. Bound in shackles of starlight, to me and my cause, now and forevermore, you shall be."

Pain ripped through my wrists as the power of her command took root in my very bones! Runes of binding, invisible to all but her and me, burned in bands across my flesh. They faded after a few breaths, but still flare up on occasion as a sharp reminder of my situation when wicked thoughts start plotting again in my brain.

"I claim you now as a prisoner, Gandersnitch, subservient to my commands and acting on your best behavior on the threat of death. I take you not as a sworn vassal, for I know that you will never swear to any, and certainly not to me. But tonight I have caught you, and though wicked you may be, from this breath forward you shall endeavor to reform. This is my wish, and thus, my command. Seek your solace in the places where the worlds mingle and meet. Be an emissary and strike the balance between dark and light. Walk the line amongst fae and men, and strive to earn my favor and thus your freedom again. You no longer must run. You are my property now, and those who break my property must surely answer to my wrath."

I was stunned. I had expected a swift death, and not a life of imposed servitude. Was it too late to fight back? Could I have broken those chains I had unwittingly allowed to be thrown about me? Tensing my muscles to spring at her, knowing I would be cut down by her men, I was stopped from attempting such rash action by a simple wave of her slender hand.

"Give him back his toys and let him leave my sight. I do not care to dally with rabble and rogues this night." Her guards were as flabbergasted as I was. Give me back my scissors and my wand? These were not mere toys and she certainly knew that as well as I did! But her men dared not disobey and I dared not to make any move at all. I knew not what game she played, but I was certain that I was now a pawn in it. I had no choice but to move to her machinations.

"You might only be a miscreant, a murderer, and a madman. Or you might be more than that, Gandersnitch. Time will tell, and I am sure to see. Now, be gone foul thing. Unless you have any words that might sway me to loosen my judgment?" There was no compassion in her eyes, no promise of redemption, and certainly no interest in what I might have to say. This was her good deed for the day, and nothing more. But thankfully, that was all I really needed it to be.

I said nothing then. I simply tipped my hat, which rankled her stewards even further, turned on my heel, and wandered off into the woods. I whistled as I went, but not because I was happy. Oh, hell no. I was not happy! I whistled to show that I was not a coward slinking away.

I was Gandersnitch the Goblin, the Bloody Barber of Goblonia, and though faerie shackles might take my freedom, they could never take away my pride.

✳ ✳ ✳ ✳

Of course, that encounter was years ago now. Not so many that I have grown old or very much reformed, nor yet earned her favor and thus my freedom. But long enough, I think, that I am able to reflect back with a clearer gaze.

I had nothing to say then, to the Queen of Faeries. But if you will indulge me for a while, tonight I have my whiskey to drink and I find my mood allows for allegory. These are my stories I tell, but they are not simply faerie tales. They are not for the faint of heart, nor for the young or the innocent. Perhaps they will help illuminate my life and my character, the reasoning behind where and what I am today. For these are my stories, dark and dangerous as they might be, and they really happened. I have the scars to prove it.

The Emperor's New Haircut

AS I SERVE MY SENTENCE at the places and times where the veils between Faerie and the human worlds grow thin, I am often asked one question by mortals, time and time again. Why, exactly, was I banished from the Goblin Realms?

The answers rendered in response to that question have been as varied as the askers. None a lie, per se, and each possessing a small kernel of the truth but never the whole story. There are so many forgotten factors that confabulate the past and thusly contribute to the warping of the present situation. And so the story changes as the memory recedes.

Perhaps here, in these pages, I can finally set the record straight. Why was I banished? In brief, murder. Murder most foul.

I have not always been the posh and admired gentleman I have become in recent years. I have, of course, always been a hobgoblin, which in and of itself lends a certain domestication and general refinement to the persona. But I was a rotten wicked bastard if the truth be told. The bloodiest barber in all the realms, that was my claim to fame. I even have the medals to prove it. Barberism was not only my profession. It was also my greatest passion.

Do you know why a barber's pole is spiraled white and red? It is a representation of the bloody bandages endemic to the trade. A barber's pole is also used to signify a brothel in some notable Asian countries. Not to claim that my pole has ever been bloodied in a brothel, mind you. Not to say that it hasn't been, either. But lest we stray too far from the point, it should be understood, I was well respected. I was in high demand. I was dangerous.

I did not have a barber shop or even a spinning pole in the grand city-state of Goblonia. I simply did not have the time to keep such an establishment, nor the inclination for settling down. I was always on the move, even then. I traveled to make my living, from duchy to fiefdom, from temple to triage, from bagnio to battlefield.

I became rich-ish, with a girl in every port, and some-times two or three. Mine was a name and a reputation that could open any door, and for those it didn't, I quickly learned how to bypass a lock with just a toothpick or a thumbscrew. This was my life, and I was thoroughly enjoying living it.

It must be said though, that I never inflicted pain upon anyone merely for the pleasure of it. It was simply part of the job. A necessary accoutrement that one must develop a professional numbness to, if one is ever to succeed in this line of work. I was a healer as much as a harmer.

You see, barbers were not always about cutting hair and trimming moustaches. We were the first surgeons; skilled with a knife and trained in the arts of bloodletting. Headaches were easily cured with a hammer to the foot or a corkscrew to the skull. Teeth were yanked, often enough the ones that actually did need to be removed. Wounds were sutured, leeches applied, boils lanced, lances boiled, and necrotic flesh hacked away with relish.

Understandable though, is the fact is that goblin surgery is often more painful than the affliction which prompted intervention in the first place. And it was very easy for undesirable nobodies to succumb to their medical issues while under the knife. So long as I was well compensated for my efforts, profitable mistakes were a distinct possibility. There is no hypocritical oath for barbers, you see. We are businessmen, not charity workers. And so it was that business eventually took me back to my beloved city of Goblonia, where a bloated, corpulent ass of a king had assumed the throne. King Rotgut, the Flatulent.

Rotgut was not born a king. In goblin society, lineage does not hold any bearing on station or status. Most of us don't even know who our parents were, and those of us that do invariably want nothing to do with them. Goblins are expected to make their own way in the world. Nothing is handed down to us and nothing is saved in reserve for our own children. Who you are, and what you have, is entirely related to what you have done for yourself.

And so it is too, with our kings. If one is strong enough, ruthless enough, or clever enough to dispose of the previous king and assume the throne... Well then, bully for you. Of course, such a crown weighs heavy on a soon to be severed head.

There had been of late growing murmurs and musings, whispered suggestions, and a drunken demand from my best friend, Grubby Wormtoe, to know why I had not assumed a kingship. The reason for that was simple. I didn't want one!

I liked my life. I had my fame, I had my fortune, and I had companionship whenever I wanted it. I didn't need a crown, and the promise of an eventual untimely end to make way for a successor was one I did not find particularly pleasant or rewarding.

King Rotgut had heard of my singular talents, however, and evidently saw me as a threat. But let's not blow this up bigger than it needs to be. He saw many people as a threat. And all of them he summoned to his court for a little chat. None were ever seen or heard from again.

So I was summoned, and so I went. I should have stayed away. it would have been easy enough, but I was prideful in my youth. Unstoppable and invincible, or so I felt at the time. Never mind that goblins are technically immortal, in so much as lobsters are. We don't die until something kills us.

I was brought before the King with all due ceremony. Which in this case meant shackled by the guards the moment I arrived at the gate, dragged through the refuse littered streets, and dumped face first before this sweaty blister of a man to learn of my fate.

"Gandersnitch the Goblin," he bellowed from a fat, froggy maw, "are you the one they call the bloody barber of Goblonia?"

I stood, dusted myself off, and gave a sweeping bow. Which was quite an accomplishment considering the fact that I was still bound in chains. "At your service, most esteemed and noble master of all the goblins."

This introduction seemed to throw him off kilter a bit, which was, of course, my plan. I wasn't atempting to kiss his arse, the mental picture of which is enough to entice anyone to take up religious orders, and there was no sniveling in my tone. It simply seemed prudent to greet him as a superior. Let him think I was in his service, so long as he knew that I was not after his crown. The damned thing would have to be heavily sanitized anyways, preferably in the fires of hell, before it was safe to be worn by the next usurper.

After a long and considering pause, in which he scratched his overflowing belly, scratched his balls (thankfully these were not overflowing and safely hidden beneath a kilt of ratty warthog fur), and then dug in his ear till he found a particularly juicy morsel before sucking it off his pinky finger with relish, he finally said, "I have heard stories of you. Is it true you know a dozen ways to kill a man?"

"Not at all, worthy king. I know exactly two hundred and thirty seven ways to kill a man. And three ways to kill a woman."

"Only three?" He snorted with surprise.

I shrugged and gave a knowing wink. "Well, my lord, there hasn't been much demand for that. Besides, there are much better things to do with women than kill them." The blank expression on his face revealed that he had no idea what those things might be. This fact alone made me breath a sigh of relief for women everywhere.

That sense of relief was cut short by his next pronouncement. "Gandersnitch the Goblin, you are a threat to my rightful claim to power. Therefore, you must die. Goodbye and have a nice day. It won't be a long one!" His guards moved towards me with rusty blood stained hatchets and a maniacal gleam in their eyes. If I did not think fast, I was done for.

"Now wait just a minute!" I exclaimed, and the king grinned ear to moldy ear. This was what he had been expecting. Begging, groveling, and pleading. He didn't get any of that though. "If you kill me now, all my secrets die with me. Including one I think you might find most invaluable."

The king held up his greasy hand, and the guards stopped their advance, just steps away from my very choppable flesh. "Tell me more," he ordered.

I adjusted my jacket, cracked my knuckles, and slipped towards the throne. Lowering my voice, so that the guards would not hear, I beckoned the king closer and murmured softly, "Truly you are the man meant for this glory. You are the rightful ruler of Goblonia, and thus all the goblin realms. I can see that clearly, but as you well know there are those who would challenge this palpability. You mistook me for one of those clueless, rebel plebeians. But never fear, I understand you concern. I have a secret that will cement your legacy for all the ages. Did you know that I also... cut hair?"

He listened closely to my words and then blinked in confusion at this revelation. Sensing my opening, I dove into it without hesitation.

"Oh yes, my noble lord. It is one of the tricks a barber of my experience picks up along the way. A sense of style. The ability to tame an unruly mane and give its bearer an undeniable aura of authenticity. And it just so happens, that in my travels, I have learned of the most imperial shingling ever known to goblinkind. It is a haircut so commanding, so demanding, that only a true king can wear it. Nay, not even a king. Only an emperor!"

"Under my skillful hand," I continued, "your power would be imitable. No one would dare question your dominance! Your grandeur would be as plain as the nose on my face. So tell me, your majesty, are you ready to be the last emperor Goblonia will ever know? Are you ready for the splendor only my scissors can reveal?"

"Yes!" Rotgut bellowed as he jumped up out of his throne to assume a triumphant stance. If, that is, triumph involves a bouncing barrel of a belly hanging down to one's knees, a quadruple chin, and sagging breasts that look like someone sculpted the Venus of Willendorf out of silly putty and left her to fester in the sun. "I shall be Emperor of all the realms!"

I stepped away, and let him have his moment. Nodding in satisfaction to the guards, I gently shooed them back to their corners with a subtle wave of my hand. "Exactly! Now we are talking. Tonight, I must sharpen my scissors and anoint them with kingly oils. Tomorrow, you will rival the stars."

"Usurp the stars!" he bellowed with gusto.

"Yes, well... That is your modus operandi, isn't it?" I muttered with a roll of my eyes.

"What did you call me?"

"Nothing insulting, my lord. It is just Latin... For, great and glorious and all that crap. Literal translation, in fact. As you said, tomorrow you will usurp the stars!"

"No... Tonight! It must be done tonight."

"Uhm... I sorta have other plans tonight. There was this gorgeous young dryad on the way in..." He turned and glared at me suspiciously. Damnit. He could not suspect that I was planning to cut and run. Which of course, I was.

"I mean, I must sharpen my scissors. They must be impossibly sharp, for this mythical haircut to succeed. You deserve, nay demand, nothing less than perfection. Am I right?"

"Completely right! Perfection suits me." And then he had me locked in the dungeon for the evening so that I could sharpen my scissors without distractions or disturbances. Clearly, there was a hair more wit to this pustule than was outwardly apparent.

And so I sharpened. And I oiled. And I sharpened some more. All through the night, without a wink of sleep. For I knew that come dawn, I must either give the best performance of my life... Or the last.

Perhaps it bears noting, for those of you who haven't already surmised the plot of this story (which was so ungratefully stolen from me in Denmark during the 19th century), that I did not know of a secret magical haircut that would secure the empire for this blighted walrus with delusions of grandeur.

There wasn't even an empire to speak of. If anything, the goblin realms were a chaotic mess of individual tribes constantly at each other's throats. And often slitting those throats to make gravy to go with the sausages.

I was, as some would say, up to my ears in a river of guano with no oars in sight. Those some, of course, are the ones who couldn't manage a proper turn of phrase if it came with its own damn merry-go-round. I was screwed. And not in a good way.

Dawn came much too early for my liking, though granted this was not a new sensation. I preferred to sleep till noon most days. But at the crowing of the cock, I was hauled back out of my cell and returned to the king's chamber without even a spot of tea or a nibble of breakfast.

I ushered away the guards and servants and barred the door, explaining to the king that my techniques must be kept absolutely secret, lest someone else prove unfaithful and use them to create a challenger to his magnificence. Dragging a chair to the middle of the room, I let the old flabby Rotgut get settled and then tied a greasy, stained tablecloth around his massive neck.

"Now remember, only a true king can handle this haircut. I know that you are the true king, and you know that you are the true king. So does it really matter what the rabble thinks? I am not saying it won't work for you, but there are stories, you know... false kings trying to don this symbol of majesty and being blasted by the forces of fate for daring such an impudent mockery of true noblesse oblige. Mythic stuff like that, Greek tragedies and all."

While I pretended to try to talk him out of it, and made certain he was aware of the dangers, I double checked my scissors to make sure they were good and sharp. Now, these scissors were not exactly magic, in so much as they did not turn the bearer invisible, or shoot fireballs, or sing Broad-way show tunes to lull giants to sleep. They were more in line with that mythical blade called Excalibur. A symbol, though not nearly as famous, and imbued with the ability to cut through just about anything, so long as it was normally cuttable.

Granted, that doesn't sound so impressive now that I write it down. I mean, certainly wars have never been fought over these scissors. And nobody ever built a round table to idealize them. The ability to cut through stuff that normal scissors can cut through already could be arguably the worst superpower ever invented, or at least a close second to that guy in the speedo who talks to fish.

But here's the rub: my scissors only required a single snip, no matter how thick or tough the cord. If it could be eventually sawed or hacked through with a barber's blade, I could do it in the blink of an eye with the merest amount of effort. And you might be surprised at how many things can actually be cut, if your blade is sharp enough.

Of course, my warnings had no effect on this pimpled tit of a king. "Nothing shall dissuade me, fool," he blustered. "I shall be emperor! It is my destiny!"

So, with a shrug and sigh, I set to work. A snip here, a snip there, and then in my frustration and despair, a bit of a slip-snip. This was promptly followed by a spray of blood and an unearthly howl of pain from the reigning king. A twisted fillet of flesh flopped to the floor. As I stooped to pick it up, the king cried out, "What is that?"

"Why... It is your ear, my lord." I could have stitched it back on, given the chance, but a plan of escape had suddenly sprung to my brain. Instead of stitches, I tossed the appendage away with a flourish of disdain, as if it were nothing more than a worthless piece of biological effluvium. "I have removed it, in the fashion of all the great emperors so you need not be bothered by the plaintive cries of your petty minions as you crush them underfoot."

He sat up straighter in his chair, blinked back the tears, and gritted his teeth though the pain. Crushing minions underfoot sounded like a good plan, and you didn't need both ears to do that.

"I mean, if you want me to stop, I certainly can," I offered gently. "Like I warned, only true kings can pull off this haircut. There is no shame in turning away from greatness, my lord. It may not sit as well on you as we had both believed."

"I am the true king! And I shall be the greatest Emperor ever known to goblinkind. Continue, you blasted barber. Continue, I say!"

And so I did. A snip here, a snip there, and then a vicious snap, this time quite intentional. Again it was followed by a spray of blood and another roar of pain from my ignoble client.

"What was that?" he snarled in outrage. I held out another floppy, flaccid slab of flesh for him to see, and then tossed it away to join its mate.

"That, my lord, was your other ear. I have removed it, in the fashion of all great kings, so that you will not hear the prattling of your advisors and underlings. As the true king, you need not be bothered by the naysaying and critiques of your lessers. I can stop though, if you wish," I offered again. "I mean, we haven't achieved empire dominating majesty yet, but we are probably close enough. A true king would see the ruse, but I understand if we must re-evaluate the situation."

"Stop? Never! I am a true king! What need have I of foolish words from those who would lead me astray? Carry on, barber! Carry on, before I flay you alive for your hesitation!"

Please do not mistake me. This was not my proudest moment. As I mentioned earlier, I do not inflict pain for pleasure. This horrible charade seemed to be my only way out of my unfortunate predicament. I think we can all agree, though, that this idiot had it coming.

And so, I continued. A snip here, a snip there, and then a mighty snap of my silver blades. Again, there was a howl, a spray of blood, and a stumpy spear of flesh falling to the floor. "What's that?" the king whimpered, his hands instinctively checking under his kilt in alarm.

"Why, it is your nose, my lord. Nothing more. I have removed it so that you need not breathe the same putrid air as the peasants. As the true king, you should only smell your own heady aroma. Shall I stop, my lord? Are you glorious enough yet?"

"Stop? Why you sniveling little rat! Do you think you will deny me my birthright? I shall have you roasted on a spit once I am emperor. Continue on, and no more delays!"

And so I did. A snip here. A snip there. One final snap. Silence... And then a soft dull thud. "What's that my lord? Why it is your head. I have removed it, so that you need not be bothered by anything but your own rotten thoughts ever again. Truly, you are a great emperor." I bowed to his corpse, wiped my blades on the blood drenched table cloth, unbarred the door, and walked right out of Goblonia with a spring in my step and a devilish grin on my lips.

I did not realize it at the time, but I was walking out of the city forever. I had just slain a king, and one that nobody else had managed to dispose of. By not assuming the throne in his place, I had destabilized the power structure of the entire realm. While grateful for my service, other kings began to worry that they would be next. I found my fame turning to infamy. Wanted posters with my likeness were tacked to every tavern and every bridge. I had become, in the tales of the time, a vengeful vigilante out for blood and justice.

My prospects were grim indeed. I was banished from courts where I had previously enjoyed lavish living and hearty welcome. I was chased from baronies by hulking ogres with wicked clubs. The warring chieftains had come together in shared animosity towards me, and they announced a sizeable reward for any who managed to bring them my head. My license to commit barberism was revoked by the guild of Goblonia, and my name slandered and smeared in every salon.

Bounty hunters came after me time and time again. And though they never succeeded in their task, I eventually grew tired of their cat and mouse game. So I left. I wandered between the realms, until I was captured and bound, as you have already read. But as luck would have it, I have never met anyone horrible enough to warrant an encore performance of my most infamous haircut. And I certainly hope that I never do. From all this trouble, I have learned a very simple fact. When separated from their shoulders, heads make such a horrible mess.

Bunny Foo Foo

NOW, BEFORE YOU BECOME overly fond of me, or imagine me to be some sort of hero that I am most assuredly not, I have a confession to make. Hopefully this will give you a true insight to my character and sway your opinion firmly toward the negative. I hate children's songs.

Bad enough are their simplistic melodies, mind numbing repetition, and thinly veiled attempt to teach a lesson. But worst of all are the untrained and squeaking voices of tiny humans singing off key and out of rhythm with their peers. Give me the banging of pots and pans over that garbage any day. This so called "singing" of sweet, cherubic innocents is nothing more than cruel and unusual punishment to my ears.

It seems to me that music teachers must have been really horrible mass murderers or some such in their past lives. Or, contrarily, they might be simply insane in this one. These options are the only ones that make any bit of sense.

So as you can see, I absolutely despise nursery rhymes and childish sing-alongs. Most of them are in fact nothing more than revisionist history, faerie propaganda, and belligerent hogwash! For instance:

Little Bunny Foo Foo
Hopping through the forest
Scoopin' up the field mice
And bopping them on the head!

Down came the Good Fairy,
And she said,
"Blah blah blah...
...something about a goon!"

This little tune used to be a quite popular children's song. But is it as innocent and well-meaning as it seems? A good fairy defending the poor field mice from a villainous rabbit? Hardly! It is nothing more than a smear campaign against yours truly, as all of the classic songs are!

"London Bridge is Falling Down?" Admittedly, maybe that one was my fault. But is it really fair to set it to music? I make one little mistake and people have to remind me of it for all eternity. It's old news. Just build a new bridge and get over it.

Or what about that other earworm people teach toddlers to sing, in an ill-fated endeavor to get them to keep their fingers occupied and thus out of their noses for a whole impossible minute, "Where is Thumbkin?" Don't look at me! How in the world would I know? I never stole a single child named Thumbkin. I never even met a child named Thumbkin. What kind of deranged parents name their child Thumbkin in the first place? Think of the issues that kid is going to have in school!

Maybe, just maybe, it is better that he got stolen away. Hopefully his new parents love him more than the original ones did, and give him a much better name. And he forgets all about those stupid twits who don't even have the forethought to check a friggin book of baby names when they discover that "Whoops! Guess I didn't take a pill that morning after all..." They should actually be thanking me for getting rid of an unexpected blight in their life. Where is that song, huh?

A goblin saved my life today!
Took this bawling brat away!
Let's all sing hip hip hooray!
A goblin saved my life today!

They weren't even married! He didn't love her! How were they going to raise a baby? Did you think he was actually going to support them both on his salary as a truck driver? And she was just some bleach blonde tart that looked good after three shots of tequila... But like I said, I never saw the child. I don't know anything.

Back to Bunny Foo Foo, the bopping field mice, and the Good Faerie. There is the smallest kernel of truth to that one, but it is not entirely what you may think. Let me explain how it really happened.

✖ ✖ ✖ ✖

1849, the last day of October. I was living in the goblin ghetto of Istanbul. It was like a market of the mad. An overturned rotting log of the ludicrous. A festering cesspool of the worst of the worst. The sort of place, where if you found yourself strolling through on a bright and sunny Sunday afternoon, perhaps on your way home from church with a holy hymn escaping your lips as a uplifting whistle, you would be lucky to escape with only your wallet missing. If you were really lucky, you might make it out of there without your wife.

Oh the wonderful sights, sounds, and smells of goblin commerce! Tents, and shacks, and hovels, and carts - all piled high with the roasting flesh of exotic animals, mounds of sweet succulent forbidden fruits, and cloth in all the strangest colors, as if a rainbow were seen through the eyes of a psychotic bumble bee.

You could find anything there that your heart desired, and lose most everything that you already had. The girls were easy, the wine was plenty, and the prices were dirt cheap! It was a carnival carousel set on high speed, with all the animals hopped up on fairy mushrooms, and the brass ring forever out of reach. But that didn't stop any of us from trying to snag it anyways.

That year it was my turn to host the annual Autumn Fright Fest, wherein my goblin expatriate friends and I dressed up in the most horrifying costumes that we could find and terrorized the city from dusk till dawn. It was much like your modern trick or treat, only with more bloodshed and less candy.

Once all my guests had arrived, drunk my cheapest rum, mingled for a bit, and had become good and riled up, I ascended to the attic to retrieve the box of costumes set aside for just such an occasion. With a passion for interesting fashion, I had been collecting the various garments in this box for years. It contained Attila the Hun's helmet, Napoleon's jacket (too short for me of course), the Wicked Witch of the East's socks (some uppity tart had stolen her fancy silver shoes), and the piece de resistance—the severed head of Marie Antoinette's second cousin's butler!

I brought this chest of wonders downstairs and set it in the middle of the floor. With a refined sense of theatrics, I blew the thick coat of dust off the lid. To let the suspense build, I slowly opened the box and stepped back dramatically. I could taste the anticipation of my friends and their impatience for the marvelous garb inside.

"Ehh. What's so special 'bout all that? Just looks like tatters and droppings to me," my best friend, Grubby Wormtoe, mumbled in consternation. He was a redcap and thus overly fond of blood, a terrible dresser, and not too bright. But in this instance, he was also correct.

Tatters and droppings indeed. And two mice sitting atop the ruins. Nay, not mice. Rats! Big rats, with beady eyes and nasty gnawing teeth. My costumes were destroyed! My years of yard sale scavenging flushed right down the drain. Enraged, I grabbed the rats by the tails and flung them out the door.

"Well, shit!" I said, allowing myself the vulgarity in light of the situation. "We don't have any scary clothes. We might have the makings of a bubonic plague in here, but we certainly aren't going to be dressed properly for it!" I was certain that the night was ruined.

But then Grubby spoke up. "Eh... I might have something." And he shambled off to retrieve his impromptu solution. "Something" is exactly what he had. Not something great. Not even something marginally good. But he did have *something*. That truth is undeniable.

The "something" that he had was seven white rabbit suits. Each with long floppy ears and a powder puff tail. I didn't ask what a redcap was doing with such attire. To be honest, I did not want to know. The details of Grubby's personal life were not something I felt comfortable prying too deeply into. It simply wasn't a pastime conducive to maintaining one's sanity. But he *had* come through in a pinch. We did have costumes, as anti-climactic as they were.

"Fine! These will do." The rest of the company looked skeptical, but I had an idea and hastily sought to assure them. "No, really. We can make these work. But we have to have some really horrible carrots!" And so, without waiting for an argument, I darted down to the root cellar to retrieve said carrots.

Now, you must understand that at this point in my life I was not yet a barber. I had not found my true calling, and was instead a confirmed bachelor. Most single young men would set out to woo as many pretty ladies as possible. However, as we all know, goblin women are patently un-wooable. They are universally green, warty, and rude.

As a result of this dearth of suitable female companionship, I was a lonely and frustrated bachelor. So I did what anyone in this situation would do: I took up gardening. Indeed, my root cellar was a thing of pride and joy. I had the ripest, rankest, reddest tomatoes, the slimiest okras, the waxiest ears of corn, and the most twisted, gnarled, and nastiest of carrots! They would do nicely for the night.

Grabbing the bunch of carrots, I marched back up the stairs and presented them proudly to my friends. They still seemed skeptical, but it took me a moment to realize why.

"Ehh... Those don't look like carrots." Grubby frowned and squinted at the bundles I held. "Too greasy. Too hairy." Greasy and hairy indeed. They were not carrots at all! They were mice. Nay, not mice. Rats!

Enormous, greasy, sewer rats, with blood red eyes and terrible yellow teeth. They were not exactly happy at being mistaken for produce and carried around by the tails, but I was none too pleased to have found them in my root cellar devouring my carrots either. I swung them over my head, once, twice, thrice, and hurled them back out the door.

"Right then! No carrots! Rabbit ears on! Everyone out!" I bellowed the commands at my friends and pointed stoically at the door as the stress of the night began to wear on my patience. I figured if we could just get out of the house and on with the revelries, then everything would end up alright. I was dead wrong.

Certainly we had a mighty fine parade, and we terrorized many an unfortunate soul that night. Grubby somehow managed to score an extra spleen and half of a chicken. It was the bottom half though, freshly cut, and it ended up running away while he was distracted by his own terrible reflection.

When we returned to my humble abode, there seemed to be some sort of chaos happening inside. My first reaction was elation, as my march had clearly been a success! I was so confident, in fact, that I assumed the elder goblins must have decided to throw an impromptu party in my honor. I flung open the door grandly and bellowed out in triumph, "My dear friends, thank you!"

Grubby, ever the oblivious one, seemed slightly taken aback. "Ehh – these are friends of yours? They look kinda shifty and small." Shifty and small indeed. The house was full of mice. Nay, not mice. Rats!

Gigantic black sewer rats with devilish bleeding red eyes of doom, and snarling, snapping yellow teeth the size playing cards, all dripping with filthy putrid ooze! They were eating my food, drinking my drinks, and leaving nasty little rat droppings all over my table and chairs.

I had had enough of this nonsense! I charged forward with murder in my eyes and a froth of rage on my lips. As it seemed a particularly fitting end to the evening, the rest of the company followed suit and a bit of a scuffle ensued. My friends were kicked at by little ratty feet. Grubby was clawed and scratched by little ratty claws. I was bitten by little ratty teeth right on the end of my nose! But in the end, we prevailed. The rats were rounded up, and hurled out into the street.

"Now stay out of here, you nasty greedy trespassers!" I snarled after them as I slammed the door closed. That should have been the end of it. We should have been able to retire in peace, drink the rest of the rum, and reminisce about adventures gone by. But fate had other ideas.

Not five minutes after ridding the house of rats there came a sharp and persistent rapping on the front door. Grubby opened it cautiously and in flitted a plus sized fairy girl without even the good breeding to wait for a "Who is it?" or a "Do come in, please." She just barged right into the parlor as if she owned the place, like a pink walrus in a tutu with absurdly small bumblebee wings and thick Coke bottle spectacles.

Her squinty piggish eyes looked me up and down disapprovingly, as she placed her hands on her hips and announced in a petulant voice, "I am the Good Fairy, Misses Lavender Fussypants. And I have received a complaint..."

She paused and frowned in confusion, then pulled a ratty feather duster from her cleavage and waved it dismissively over my costumed form. Batting me in the face with the duster, she squealled, "Mr. Bunny— Foo Foo!" Clearly, this woman was insane.

"Uhm... Excuse me? My name is Gandersnitch the Goblin, and this is my house!" I was in no mood for games, and certainly not from the dregs of self-righteous fairy folk. "What in the hell are you talking about?"

"Good Fairy, eh? Only one of ya left? Can I get your autograph?" Grubby chuckled in simple minded merriment.

I rolled my eyes and sounded a snort of derision at his joke. "I wonder what sort of credentials it takes to get that job, eh?" I elbowed Grubby in the side and then turned my attention back to our latest imposter "Aren't you supposed to have a badge or something? Or at least a warrant to barge into my home at this hour, uninvited, unannounced, and unwelcomed? Clearly you have the wrong house, anyways. Let me show you to the door."

The fat fairy balked at my efforts to remove her, and her considerable bulk proved quite resistant to my shoves. "Mr. Bunny Foo Foo..." Again she batted me in the face with her duster. "I have a whole family of field mice that just knocked on my door crying about the horrible treatment they received at your hands! Bopping them on the heads! Why would you do such a horrible thing? Those poor, sweet mice!"

I was so confounded by her story that I gave up my attempts to escort her out and simply stared, agape, for a whole twenty seconds. When I finally found my wits, I resisted the rising urge to hurl obscenities, and instead managed to respond with a level yet biting tone.

"Clearly, Miss Pantywad, you need new glasses. You also are way out of your jurisdiction here. I've bopped no mice. Not a single one. I have, however, had a very trying night. And if you don't scram by the count of three, I am going to bop you upside the head!"

This threat seemed to have done the trick. Her eyes went wide with shock at my promise of violence, and tears rolled down her face as she cried out, "You horrible horrible.... Goon!" She tossed the disheveled duster at my head and then ran from my home, crying and wailing like a stuck pig.

Her retreat did not bother me one bit. Frustrated and exhausted, I slumped down in my overstuffed chair by the fire and reached for the rum. Grubby ushered himself and the rest of the guests out the door and shut it securely closed behind him. Finally there was peace. No rats, no meddling faeries, and no worries.

This reprieve, however, was only to last till the next morning. As I took my daily stroll down toward the docks, to see if perhaps the tide had washed in any impressionable and lonely young nymphs, I heard the alarming cry of a newsmonger. "Little Bunny Foo Foo, hopping through the forest, scooping up the field mice and bopping them on the head! Full story at eleven!"

And that was all it took. A horde of rats, one meddling overstuffed tart, and a catchy phrase that could be set to music. Over the next few months, that annoying song became the hit of the town. There was no escaping it! Everywhere I went, it could be heard. Mocking me, taunting me. My wretched revelry didn't go down in the books as the best one ever, after all. Instead, I was recorded in the collective sub-consciousness of little children everywhere as a rabbit and a goon!

I did the only thing a man in my position could do. I gave up on finding love. I gave up on gardening, and culture, and the ghetto of Istanbul. I returned to the land of my birth, and in this disenfranchised state, I discovered my true calling: bloodshed, rumours, and revenge. I became the barber you know me as today, the bloodiest barber in all of the Goblonia.

✖✖✖✖

The Goblin Queen

WE HAVE ALL HEARD the tripe about where faeries come from, right? A mildly famous author once wrote, "When the first baby laughed for the first time, its laugh broke into a thousand pieces, and they all went skipping about, and that was the beginning of fairies." Fanciful imagery, for sure, but clearly this Mr. Barrie was not up to date on modern sexual education.

Faeries come from the same place that goblins do. And goblins come from the same place human children come from. And human children come from the same place that babies of almost every other animal come from. I hope that I do not have to paint you a clearer picture than that.

Of course, I do understand where the confusion begins. We don't like to talk about the gory details with outsiders, any more than you do. Have you ever seen any goblin women? They are downright disgusting! So perhaps you can imagine the sights and smells associated with globs of warty green flesh, all slick with sweat and blood, repeatedly slapping against each other? Actually it is probably best if you don't imagine that. It is terrible mental image indeed!

The interesting thing is, that unlike animals in the mortal realm, the concept of mythical mating doesn't so much depend on random chance and compatible DNA. Basically, if the bits fit, no matter how much mashing and gnashing is required to do so, then a bouncing baby amalgamation is ultimately inevitable.

Simply look to the minotaur, the centaur, or the harpy for examples of people getting freaky with animals in an enchanted realm. Thankfully, things like that are only possible on our side of the veil. Otherwise you human sorts would have a plethora of wooly, bleating Scotsmen.

So, how do we answer the question of "Where do babies come from?" The same way most humans do: misinformation, denial, and outright lies. We don't treat the topic as taboo, per se, we just choose never to raise the possibility of sex as an option in the first place. Perhaps one day a young goblin will wind up in the midst of a satyrical orgy and hopefully figure things out for themselves. But without the cultural tie in to connect the intersection of dangly bits of anatomy with the generation of offspring, we are usually pretty safe.

As a youth, I had heard the propaganda that faeries spread claiming that they come from laughter and moonbeams. And that goblins come from mud, or labyrinths, or gas station bathrooms. Indeed, I believed there was a kernel of truth to all that, as we have all heard of the great goblin labyrinth of old and the human child in the striped pajamas who escaped its clutches. The goblin child in this story did not come from a labyrinth, though. She came from an egg, or at least that is what I thought at the time.

It had been explained to me that lots of goblins came from eggs. When the egg man came to town, there were always a few eggs that didn't get eaten, and so they started to rot. Curious creatures as we goblins are, especially in regards to nasty smells, these rotten eggs were inevitably cracked open to find out what was within that smelt so wonderfully foul. Inside one would sometimes find a wriggling wormy creature, mostly head with a fat body and a slimy little tail. This was a goblin baby, resembling nothing more than an overgrown tadpole—with teeth.

You see, when goblin children are born, they all look mostly the same. Sure, some might be a bit bigger, or a bit louder, or a bit greener, browner, or yellower. But they are all still identifiable as baby goblins. But one day, one egg, was born a bit different.

I imagine that this particular egg was fancy, all shimmery blues and greens and silvers, with a pinch of glitter sprinkled over the top. And inside there was not a wormy thing of green or brown or yellow, but a pinkish thing, with arms and legs already, and even a tuft of purple hair.

As you might well imagine, goblins are forced to grow up pretty fast, as our society is careless, rude, and dangerous. One must learn all the important things about being a goblin in the early years, and then get on out into the world to make our own way. It is not like our parents are going to do anything for us after all. Goblins make terrible parents!

And so it was for the little pink goblin child with purple hair. She was bustled off at only a few days old to the goblin school, as was I, and it is there that our paths first crossed. But it was not an easy or happy time for her, as she was so very different from all the rest of us. For one, she was the wrong color. For two, she was small and slender and delicate. For three, she had that amazing purple hair. These things made her a prime target for bullying and pranks. Which, of course, I participated in wholeheartedly.

Often in such difficult circumstances, the outcast will prove to be exceptionally good at something and will use the constant adversity to catalyze into a veritable genius. Maybe they will become a great scholar, or sports star, or insanely adept at hiding in lockers and garbage cans. However, it was not to be so with that dear little waif. She was absolutely terrible at everything goblins did.

In nose picking class, she failed to produce a single flickable booger. Her nose was just too small for proper digging. In belching class, all she could manage was a slight hiccup. In farting class, she never even

The little pink goblin ventured out, as was expected of all her classmates, and though I was not with her, I did discover the details of her transformation many years later. She climbed the Cliffs of Calamity, but her hands were too weak to chisel out horns. So instead she charmed those rabid mountain goats and gathered up their wool. She spun it into thread, and wove the thread into cloth, and dyed the cloth in the river of unmentionable filth that flowed from the cliffs. Eventually she had herself a very nice psychedelically colored dress. It was bit scratchy, but with incredible swirls of electric yellow, neon orange, and acid green.

Next she went to the swamp, but her eyes would not fall out, no matter how hard she whacked herself in the back of the head. I always rather liked the eyes she had anyways. They were not grey and worn out like ours, but were a sparkling bright lavender color instead. So she kept her eyes and instead plucked the wings off one of the giant flies and stuck those on her own back with some sticky swamp muck.

Lastly she travelled to that forest of doom, but evidently could not bring herself to pluck down a tail. Perhaps the cries of the animals trapped above were too piteous and she could not bear to add further to their suffering. Besides that, none of the tails really looked all that good with her purple hair. Of course, I had no such qualms and found a quite fabulous tail on my own journey to adulthood.

As she was puzzling over her conundrum with the tails, one of the grasping evil trees evidently became a bit too forward, so she smacked off the offending branch and from it whittled a magical wand. Satisfied with her own new look, which was almost exactly the same as the one she started with, off she went into the world to make something of herself. To be honest though, we all figured she would not amount to much more than an appetizer for a hungry ogre.

Not being terribly clear with her geography, she wandered deeper into the forest and it wasn't long before she came to a tree filled with tiny twinkling lights. Not only twinkling lights, but also tiny pinkish goblins much like herself. They even had wings like hers!

These tiny pink goblins invited her to join them at a feast for dinner. It was all fruits and sweets and wine, but she was just happy to be invited to a party, as this had never happened to her before. And she practically dripped with desperation to be accepted amongst her new found friends, so she did not mind so much their strange choice of food. It was her yearning to belong, that prompted her to show this newly discovered tribe of tree goblins that she could indeed be all that a goblin is supposed to be.

At dinner, she managed to pick the biggest booger anyone had ever seen, and flicked it right at the princess of the tree. Her new friends were mortified. Sadly, it still wasn't big enough to impress them.

After she ate a bit more and fidgeted with the hem of her dress, she finally summoned up her courage to try again. As the prince of the tree stood to make a toast in her honor, she replied with the biggest combination belch and fart anyone has ever heard. It was fantastic! The pink "goblins", however, thought this was horribly rude and most undignified.

Growing ever more frustrated at her failed attempts to fit in, she tried once more to win their approval. Climbing on the table, she roared loudly and made the most horrible snarl anyone has ever seen. The pink goblins darted away in complete terror.

Dejected and alone once more, she trudged back home to our goblin town where we had forgotten all about her due to a bit of trouble of our own. The village was all unsettled, as a troll had invaded and set up camp smack in the center of the market square. He was eating all the food, drinking all the rum, and fouling the well as he soaked his pustulated backside in our drinking water.

I don't know what overcame her, but something queenly inside her soul snapped when she saw this monster, and she stood up straight and fierce to face him down! Her sparkling eyes burned with a hidden fury and her purple hair crackled in the air. Before anyone could stop her, she flew right up to that troll, smacked him in the nose with her wand, and yelled at him to get the hell out of the village.

A spray of glitter shot out of the wand, which caught both the girl and the troll completely by surprise. She dropped the wand in astonishment. He, however, started to sneeze, as trolls, like many darker fae folk, are terribly allergic to glitter. He sneezed. And he sneezed again. And he continued to sneeze himself right out of town.

That pink little goblin girl was suddenly a hero! She had saved our people, in a way none of us would ever have considered. Sure, she was a different color, and not warty in the least, and slender and curvy, and wearing a really gorgeous and rather revealing gown. These facts slowly dawned on the men in our village, and they began to experience funny stirrings of emotion in their nether regions. One by one, they declared their undying devotion to her soft, delectable, and entirely ungoblin-like body.

This development did not sit so well with the matrons of our tribe, and so the goblin women quickly huddled together and decided to chase the little pink tart right out of town. The menfolk, however, had already made her a tinsel and barbed wire crown and offered her dominion over all of them.

The little pink goblin girl, the one everyone had shunned and made fun of and laughed at, had now been abruptly coronated as our queen! She stood there astonished and confused, suddenly elevated by those that had always reviled her. And then those same subjects started arguing over who would get to wed her, bed her, and become the King. I wasn't even considered as a likely candidate for the position.

As the villagers argued and plotted amongst themselves, she quirked her brow, turned her head, and spat out a huge, nasty glob of phlegm. She tossed that absurd crown to the rubbish pile and shouted angrily at the arguing opportunist villagers, "Go screw yourself! I am not putting up with any of you anymore! " Then she stalked off into the world alone.

The end. That's it. Though honestly, I suspect she was probably a lesbian anyways. Faeries often are. We crossed paths again many years later, and I must say that I count myself very lucky. Yes, she was pretty. Yes, she could fly. But she turned out to be a rather terrible kisser.

Of Trolls & Tribulations

YOU MIGHT BE under the assumption that the worst of my troubles took place before my capture by the Faerie Queen. However, you would also be quite mistaken. My life has seen a fair share of drama since then as well, usually of my own making. Though in my defense, and in this particular instance, I must place the blame squarely on the dress.

"Hey sexy. The griffin says 'Hello'." It was the oddest pick up line I had ever heard.

It came from a delicious black haired waif, who was trying just a bit too hard to appear sultry and vampish. Her powder pale skin was marred with a spray of freckles, though a reasonably luscious effect was achieved by her smoky eyeshadow, black manicured nails, and a low cut black dress. Very low cut! The narrow V of the neckline dropped all the way to her navel, giving a tantalizing glimpse of milky flesh and bantam cleavage. All in all, it was a rather provocative garment, the likes of which would be right at home in a "Halloween Harlots and Vixen Villainesses" edition of the Froderick's of Harrowood catalogue.

I had never met this girl before and I have not seen her again since that night. I honestly can't even remember what her name was, if she ever told it to me at all. Really though, how could I be expected to recall any such insignificant details when presented with that dress? It is no wonder I managed to miss the girl's message. The actual message, I mean. The sexual communication was rather clear.

Now, lest you think I frequent places where such attire is common place, I should perhaps point out that this was a special occasion. (And not simply for what followed that evening with the girl in the low cut black dress.) This was an occasion featuring gobs of girls in garments of similar seductivity. Plenty of mortals, mingling amongst the Fae, exalting in simple vices to the pounding beat of a gypsy band called something about a Punky and the French. This my friends, was a Dark Faerie ball.

Such exhibitions are a relatively modern phenomenon. They were started by mortals as an excuse to have a borderline classy party in which the participants flirt with the ideals of the Unseelie, but with no true commitment required on anyone's part. They are normally relatively tame affairs when compared to the depraved revelries of a traditional

Goblinmoot, but serve as a suitable endeavor for the more subtle of the mythic folk to mingle, meet and, in some cases, seek out their next meal. By unspoken agreement these gatherings are neutral ground for creatures like us. They are a chance to pass messages, spy on old foes, and inspire new prodigies to greatness. And perhaps spend a few hours bathing in the warmth of some mortal trollop who will be nothing more than decaying bones beneath the earth in a few decades time whilst we will still be living it up, safe and sound and forgetting their names. If we are lucky, that is.

For those however, that are not terribly lucky or quite as suave as I am (and let's face the facts here, not many of my kind are), chances are you will wind up alone at the bar, nursing an overpriced beer, and being viewed as a strange creeper by pretty much everyone you meet. Though that night my sympathy was lacking, seeing as how I had told Grubby time and time again that most mortal girls don't care for the sight or smell of fresh blood, regardless of a redcap's own cultural norms pertaining to fancy dress parties.

Normally I might deign to comfort my best friend in such straits, but let us not forget, I had a little black dress on my arm. Grubby could wait. He would understand, and if the tables had been reversed (which, strangely enough, has never happened, unless you count the time we literally did reverse the tables to create chaos amongst the wait staff and guests at the wedding of the Archduke Ferdinand), he would expect the same begrudging accommodations from me. As it turns out, he did quite fine on his own that night, and wound up as the champion of an impromptu game of bloody knuckles with a morose violinist he found wandering alone in the garden.

After several drinks (mine being the classic standby of a rusty nail, though mortal bartenders these days balk at serving it with an actual nail), a handful of tall tales which caused much giggling and left my date's dark lady facade shattered on the stained carpet of the hotel bar, and an intoxicated kiss which indicated quite clearly that she was not used to drinking at all, let alone in the company of goblins, I signaled the bartender for the check, left a handsome tip, and slipped towards the elevator with the black dress tugging me playfully along.

Clearly, I was not thinking or paying attention to much of anything, save my mortal companion and her dress. Mostly her dress, as I cannot even recall now the color of her eyes. My immediate attentions were on how to keep her from puking in the potted topiaries or tumbling over the balcony, and if I had had my proper wits about me, I most likely would have paid the bill in faerie gold. But I was in a mood of pleasant anticipation and willful ignorance. That, unfortunately, is no excuse. I really should have noticed the printed message at the bottom of the check.

```
      The GRIFFIN says HELLO.
         Thank YOU and
      Please COME again NOW.
```

I am not going to bore you with the details of the rest of that wicked evening. In part because a gentleman never kisses and tells, and neither do I. In part because I have quite honestly forgotten the intimate details of that sordid tryst due to the rather horrible shock that came afterwards. But mostly because once the dress had been tossed in the corner and was thus no longer in the picture, the enchantment it inspired fell rather flat.

I am sure she was pretty. And drunk, of that I am positive. And she evidently had a thing for long noses. But as is usually the case, the wrapping on the package was much more intriguing than the gifts it concealed beneath. This is a truth often forgot in these modern times; things left to the imagination are almost always more exquisite than the harsh reality served up on a silver platter like the carcass of a dead trout. The harsh reality I awoke to before dawn the next morning made sure I was not about to miss the message for a third time.

Instead of drowsily waking to the afterglow of each other's company, blurry memories of attempted midnight acrobatics, and morning breath, I was suddenly yanked from the oft bleached sheets by a big meaty fist encircling my rather crushable windpipe. Attached to said fist was a hairy tattooed arm that could have easily been mistaken for that of a gorilla. A bit further along, past the shoulder and sitting squat on a thick unwashed neck was the brutish face of a disgruntled ogre in a bowler hat. Morning breath at this point would have been much preferable to his natural foul stench.

"Something wrong with yer ears, Snitch? THE GRIFFIN SAYS HELLO!" Spittle flew from his mouth, as he shook me hard and then slammed me against the wall several times for good measure. The leavings of last night's dinner dislodged from his cracked yellow teeth and crawled off under the bed to die in peace. I was not so lucky.

Then it hit me! Perhaps the lack of oxygen to the brain helped the memory cut right through everything else that was cluttering up my noggin. At that moment, the girl, formerly in the black dress, didn't matter. The night before didn't matter. Grubby didn't matter. Even this ugly oversized interloper didn't matter, so long as he let go of my neck at some point in the near future to allow me a gulp of breath. I was in far deeper trouble.

I wheezed for air as best I could, and was summarily dropped the seven feet to the floor below. Hastily I grabbed my trousers, my vest, and my shoes, and threw them on in mostly the right order. Tossing a brush through my hair, for it would not do to meet the Griffin in a rumpled state, I took a quick glance in the mirror and adjusted the cap on my head. With a nod to the ogre, I pushed aside the hotel hangers and followed him into the closet.

Maybe I should have spared a glance of remorse back at the still sleeping waif. I'd be lying if I said I did that though. She would get over me. Heck, I probably did her a huge favor by not lingering, when you really stop to think about it. Not every mortal girl can handle the reality of waking up next to a hobgoblin.

Once the closet door was shut firmly behind us, the passage to the Goblin Realms opened up before us. Onward we clambered into that wretched den of sin, the Aerie of the Griffin, the most notorious crime lord in all of the Goblin Realms. The favor I owed that damnable villain was finally being called in.

✘ ✘ ✘ ✘

Mythologically speaking, a griffin is a fierce animal with the back half of a lion, and the head, wings, and talons of a giant eagle. Assuredly carnivorous and terribly competent in combat, they are often viewed as the noblest of beasts and feature prominently in the heraldry of European families. The only similarity between these creatures and the gent who claimed their moniker was the relish with which he would rip the flesh from his still living prey with his bare teeth. That, and his propensity to shit on those beneath him.

This Griffin, the one to whom I owed a favor, was a dwarf. And not just a dwarf, but a dwarf amongst dwarves. He was a beardless bastard (he could grow facial hair of course, but he kept his ugly mug close shaved to signify his rejection of his racial heritage), a runt, and a cripple with gnarled claw-like hands. This last feature was what earned him the name and to play along with the imagery he had entitled his abode, "The Aerie."

His twisted hands were entangled in every sort of illicit dealings one could imagine: drug smuggling, contraband weapons, industrial sabotage, money laundering, spying, assassination, loan sharking, and of course, human trafficking. Like a spider in the center of his web, he had contacts in every aspect of society and each one owed him a favor. This was how he managed to stay on the top of the heap, never beholden to anyone, but with an axe of debt swinging over the necks of practically everyone he knew. He had a knack for calling in those favors at the least opportune times, for the indebted that is, and absolutely no qualms against bumping off those who tried to avoid his reckoning.

Now, some of you may still be harboring the deluded notion that this is a sappy modern fairy tale, and that the Griffin was merely misunderstood. Maybe on the inside he was really a nice guy, lonely and heartbroken, and yearning to be loved. Maybe all his nastiness was simply a product of self-defense towards an inhospitable social landscape and a culture that looked down on those weaker and deformed. And I bet you think elves are beautiful, noble, and kind hearted as well. Yeah, not so much. The Griffin ate babies for breakfast.

In addition, an aerie should perhaps support the imagery of lofty heights, lush breezes, abundant sunshine, and a right comfortable nest - Griffin's abode fit exactly none of these descriptions. For starters, it was deep underground and it smelled pretty damned awful. It was also nigh impenetrable to outsiders who did not have an invitation to be there. Like the bull in Minos' labyrinth, Griffin sheltered behind a maze of switchbacks, dead ends, and terminal delays. Curiously enough, an entire black market culture had grown up in the twisting tunnels that surrounded his ante-chambers. There were stalls and slaves and blood sports of all shapes and sizes; and so long as the boss man got his cut, he did not begrudge the leeches their livelihood.

It was through this maze of sin and vice that my guide and I descended. Once or twice we became thoroughly turned around, but I was quite capable of breaking the male stereotype and asking for directions. My reputation preceded me of course, even into these dark corners of the realms, and there was nary a soul who wished to stand in my way. Sure it may have taken a bit of silver slid surreptitiously across a few palms to find the shortcuts we desired, but eventually we got where we wanted to be. Scratch that—where we were wanted to be. Personally, I would have preferred to have still been in bed. But the undeniable fact of the matter was this: I owed the Griffin a favor, and it was unhealthy to refuse his summons. I was already a wanted goblin, I didn't fancy being a dead one as well.

We finally arrived in his lair round about dinner time. My stomach was grumbling, as I had missed breakfast on this journey, and there had been no discussion regarding a stop for lunch along the way. Delays would have only made the inevitable more difficult to deal with.

"You're late, Gandersnitch. And I don't like to be kept waiting. It makes me gassy. Irritable. Prone to rash action." The Griffin was seated at a table, a ring of smoke clouded the air around him, and a slew of still wriggling minnows swam on a plate before him. Two bare chested harpy girls leaned over from either side, slipping the slimy fish into his grinning maw. In the background, barely seen from the shadows, were an assortment of lackeys and bodyguards. He was clever enough to know that I was most likely armed, which of course I was, with both my wand and my scissors, but I wasn't desperate enough to try anything stupid just yet. This was business, plain and simple. And the sooner we were done with it, the better.

I gave him a shrug and replied with a wicked grin, "Late I might be. But you are an ugly, sinful bastard. Who's to judge which is the worser crime? Not I! Especially when there are ladies involved."

He chuckled darkly and waved his own gals away. I almost felt sorry for them, being tied to such a slug. But they were harpies, and it doesn't do to pity those who are known for dragging unwilling menfolk away into their nests for horribly violent mating rituals. I should probably be pitying him instead, but I didn't. I figure some folks have to take it where they can get it.

"Ladies involved. Yes." The Griffin leered knowingly. "The girl in the black dress. You always did have a soft spot for the mortal women. Too bad she wasn't more efficient in delivering her message."

"I would counter that she was overly efficient. But the sincerest apologies are offered if my natural charm managed to derail her from her assigned course. It is not her fault she did not send me quickly on my way. Nor is it mine for dallying." I pulled out a chair and sat down, determined to keep my cool in this exchange and unbalance him, if I could manage it. A raised brow at my liberties hinted that I had achieved my goal. It remained to be seen, however, if it was wise to be so bold.

"So Gandersnitch," the dwarf began slowly, drawing out the words as if setting up some major theatrical reveal. "How are those scissors I secured for you, all those ages ago? Still sharp, as promised? Still drinking in the blood of tyrants and fools?"

An irritated sigh escaped my lips and I reached out for one of his nasty fish. I had no intention of eating it, but I felt the foolish need to push my luck. "Duller than this conversation, Griff. As always, I fear you overstated your abilities."

A sharp three tined fork slammed down into the table and only barely missed my fingers. That was only because I hastily drew them back, once I realized that I had gone a hair too far.

"Lies!" He bellowed. "But I expect nothing less from you 'Snitch. Running to hide with the Faeries. Turning your back on all that you were. Reformed, ehh? A chained pansy and a mewling coward is more like it." The dwarf was clearly not pleased. His clawed hand relinquished the fork, as it was stuck well and good into the wood, and a loud fart escaped from his rump as he snatched up another of those nasty fish.

Those were fighting words indeed, and for a moment my hand strayed to my wand. But I relented after catching the ripple of muscles from the body guards in the shadows. I wasn't going to be winning any fights in here.

"Enough sparring." I pushed my chair back and rose to my feet. "We both know I owe you a favor. And I aim to pay up. So name it already and be done. I warn you though, unless you have a way of unlocking my shackles, I am afraid that murder is right off the table."

"Oh... But I do, old friend. Of course I have ways of unlocking anything." His voice dropped to a tantalizing whisper, the gleam in his eyes betraying his cleverness and greed. And I will admit, that for a moment I was tempted to dig myself deeper into his debt. But I stood firm, for better or for worse.

"Name your favor, Griffin. I must live with my sins and so must you. But I will no longer live in your debt. What is it you want? Kidnapping? Maiming? Arson? Theft? Spit it out man, I haven't got all day to lounge around here, as un-charming as the company may be."

The villain leaned back in his chair, having won this round and knowing that the match was clearly his. "Nothing so crude, Snitch." He motioned to the shadows, and a burly fellow stepped forward with a large empty sack slung over one shoulder like a hobo Santa Claus. "I simply need you to pick up a package for me and bring it back here. Harmless, easy, discreet. You can manage that. Can't you, old friend?"

✖ ✖ ✖ ✖

And that is how I found myself in the freezing cold at twelve minutes to midnight, standing at an ancient crossroads marked with a Soviet era monument, holding an oversized rucksack and waiting for a troupe of delivery trolls. I had been there since sunset, with no company save an overly curious raccoon that had wandered by early on. I shared a bit of my dinner with it. Whiskey. Which in hindsight was quite possibly a mistake. Evidently the masked varmint was not a very experience drinker. After only a few shots, he hopped up on his hind legs, ran around in a circle three times waving his little arms, smacked into the base of the monument, threw up at my feet, and then promptly passed out cold.

I had no clue as to what I was supposed to be collecting, only that the trolls would be bringing it to me tonight. And that it would most definitely fit in my sack. I almost suspected an ambush or a double cross, which would be ironic happening at an actual point where two roads crossed, but such things weren't exactly the Griffin's style. Sure, I had insulted him, but not so much that my life was forfeit; at least I hoped not. That would just be bad for business. His and mine both.

I was pretty sure I had the right crossroads. I had followed the directions given, and the concrete monument above me matched the description. It was comprised of four huge triangles, concrete but peppered with seemingly random holes of different sizes, like giant slices of ancient Swiss cheese. The main points of the triangles touched the ground and the shorter sides joined together about twenty feet above to create a square opening in the center. They straddled the crossroads like a minimalistic origami crane. Or maybe a mutant crane with four wings. Whatever, the point is that it was really damn weird!

The monument had been there for as long as anyone could remember. Nobody knew who built it, or why; and quite honestly, nobody really cared. I could make up some believable sounding story about the points being a compass rose delineating the possible directions my future could take and the holes being the absence of compassion and humility in my life. But that's a load of poppycock, and I would rather just leave it to future English teachers to force such nonsense down your throats than to belabor it here.

It was cold. I was lonely. The raccoon was snoring. And it was starting to snow. This was perhaps, a perfect time for reflection. Maybe my current situation was a metaphor for my entire existence. What had brought me to this point, and was it all worth it in the end?

Some of you may be wondering how I wound up in debt to the Griffin in the first place. It wasn't gambling debts, and it wasn't a woman... at least, not directly. No, what I had desired, and the Griffin had acquired, was a pair of scissors.

I can already hear you rolling your eyes at my folly, but these were no ordinary scissors! I had requested scissors big enough, and sharp enough, to cut off a man's head in one snip. And indeed, as you know, they worked like a charm! So was it worth it? The tools of infamy in exchange for the momentary discomfort of waiting around in the snow for a bunch of stone brained trolls?

Thankfully, I did not have to answer that question just then, as my musings were interrupted by the creaking of wagon wheels and the slap of unshod feet on the icy road. Peering into the swirling flurry I could just make out the forms of several lumbering trolls pulling a large cart laden with heavy chests. Finally, the moment I had been waiting for had arrived. I could collect the package and get back to my own troubles by morning. Hopefully these troubles included more balls and black dresses, and fewer surprise wake up calls.

I waited in the shadows of the crossroads monument until the trolls were within striking distance. Once they were almost upon me, I stepped out into the snow and flashed my most charming smile.

"Well hello, gentlemen! Right on schedule, as always, I see." I kept the scorn and sarcasm carefully absent from my voice, or so I hoped. "Are you hungry? There is a fresh raccoon right over here. It won't take us but a minute or two to whip up a nice warming stew."

The trolls shuffled to a halt and looked up from their burden with confusion and distrust in their eyes. They were not dressed for the weather, being common laboring trolls with no more to their names than the rags they wore around their waists. Even with their thick skin and thicker skulls, it was clear that they were freezing. Steam rose from their breath and the sweat on their brows froze quickly into an icy crust. The offer of a hot meal was certainly a tempting distraction. I hated to betray my momentary companion to their hunger, but he wasn't going anywhere and his family should be happy to know that his death served a good cause.

"We suppos'da bring dis to'da dwarfs." One of the trolls spoke up, frowning with the effort of explaining himself. He glanced to his companions for support, and they nodded slowly in agreement. Then all eyes drifted hungrily back to the raccoon.

I was confident that this would be an easy exchange, so long as I walked the line between confusion and frustration without slipping. Giving a reassuring smile, I held up my index finger to clarify for them. "Dwarf, singular. And yes, I know. But it was so cold out tonight that he sent me in his stead. Not to worry chaps, we can just trade off the goods and you all can get right on to resting and feasting."

"He?" the lead troll muttered, still not entirely sure of what was going on. Cleary, he was expecting a different sort of arrangement. I was going to have to spin it out quickly.

"Well, yes..." I said knowingly. "He. I am almost positive that all dwarves are, in fact, referred to in the masculine. Have you ever seen a female dwarf?"

The trolls shook their heads slowly, confirming that I was right. Nobody has ever seen a female dwarf.

I am thoroughly convinced that they simply do not exist. Which would explain so much about the general grumpiness and lack of hygiene among my bearded brethren.

"There you have it! He it was. He it is. And he it always will be, now and forever. Amen. So, friends... business first of course, and then you can dig in. What is it that you have in your cart?" I clapped my hands together and nudged the drunken raccoon with my shoe to show that it was still quite fresh.

"Dis all da gold. For da bridge. To da dwarfs." He reached over and opened one of the chests, revealing the innards to be full to the brim with gold and jewels. My heart sunk as my frustrations soared. What in the world had I gotten myself into? The Griffin was expecting me to bring back a whole cart load of riches. And of course all the bastard gave me to carry it in was a bag.

"No, no, no... I mean, yes. Yes, of course. The gold is for the dwarves. But you see, my cart actually broke down... on the way... and the ox died... and Joe was bit by a rattlesnake... and my wife got dysentery... so we had to shoot her... wasting the bullets we needed for the deer..." The suspicion on the trolls' faces melted away into confusion once more.

"So I need to borrow your cart. I can't carry it all by myself. Of course I should pay you for the rental of said cart. So I can get the gold back to the dwarves, as promised." I shrugged and nudged the animal with my toe again. "Raccoon stew?"

The troll snorted and shook his head. "Cart not for you. Cart for trolls. Pay too much gold for da bridge already. Trolls keep cart. You carry gold. Can't carry? No problem. We just take da extra back home!" He chuckled and nodded to his fellows. There was some cleverness in that rocky skull after all or, at the very least, ingrained cruelty.

"Fine!" I grumbled, not relishing the thought of the long journey home now, not in the least. "Just empty the chests into the damn bag already. I can't feel the end of my nose anymore and if we sit here gabbing all night, then the whole lot of us will be snowmen by sunrise." I tossed the bag on the ground and tromped back under the shelter in irritation. I might have to drag the bag all night, but I wasn't about to break a sweat filling it.

The trolls made short work of emptying the contents of the cart into my sack. They were good at tossing, dumping, and schlepping. In fact, that is really the only thing trolls are ever good for. And once the bag was filled, they sat down to squabble over the raccoon. Seeming to forget entirely about turning it into a stew, they were now arguing over who got to eat the head, who got the middle, and who was stuck with the tail.

Gripping the end of the bag, which was now filled to the brim and bulging heavily on the ground, I took a deep breath and lurched forwards. And I promptly fell flat on my face in the snow!

I had been expecting a great deal of resistance from all that treasure stuffed inside, as it is a well-known fact that gold is heavy. But my bag was still as light as if it were empty. Sputtering and wiping snow from my face, I glared at the trolls and then opened the sack to see what sort of trickery this was. My instincts told me that the gold must simply be an illusion.

But it was all real! Inside the bag, the gold had substance and weight. I even bit the edge of a coin to be certain. Solid, and not simply the wispy stuff of dreams. I grabbed the bag once more and carefully tested its weight again. Light as a feather! Well alright, more than a feather. Light as an empty bag. Clearly there was magic at work here. But the magic was in the bag, not in the treasure.

Giving a cackle of delight, and waving my curt goodbyes to the trolls, I hoisted the sack of treasure and set off swiftly into the snowy night. Within the hour the "package" was safely back in the greasy clutches of the Griffin, may his black soul rot for all eternity. But more importantly, I was back home by morning. And my debt to that cunning crime lord was settled. I could spend my days in peace and relaxation. Or at least that was the plan.

✖ ✖ ✖ ✖

It took a few days for the news to circulate. Tensions had to rise, rumors had to be confirmed, and blame had to be placed. Thankfully I had not been identified, so my involvement in the whole fiasco had gone entirely unnoticed. Until now, that is, as I have filled you in on the particulars of my crime.

Hopefully, since things are calm once more, this will be nothing more than an amusing anecdote told in nursing homes and around campfires.

I saved the newspaper clippings, the first ones from when the full gravity of the situation had become clear, and I think perhaps this one will serve as the appropriate ending for my tale. It stands to reason that history, and the courts, should see that I am completely blameless in any accusations that arise. I was simply an innocent bystander that happened to be in the right place at the wrong time. So what if, technically, I did happen to start the Second Troll War?

!!! WAR HAS BEGUN !!!

GOBLONIA - What started as a simple dispute over payments owed between the nations of the Dwarves and the Trolls, has now escalated to the exchange of blows and the loss of lives. The crux of the matter is a disagreement over a single payment for bridge repairs that the Trolls say was delivered as promised to the Gongol Crossroads. The Dwarves claim to have been stood up with no recompense save the bones of a dead raccoon, which was not the agreed upon fee for service. When prompted to provide a receipt to support their claims of payment in full, the Trolls in question stormed off in a huff. Their bridge was repossessed three days later, and the Troll families living there were evicted.

In protest of this 'unfair treatment' other Troll tribes have begun to refuse to make payments that were due, and in turn the Dwarves have been seizing more bridges and evicting the occupants. Thud Thudson was quoted as saying, "Stinking squatty Dwarfs! Why they want old bridge? They live in mines! Now where we gonna live? Me punch next Dwarf I see inna face!" Which he did.

The Dwarven company of 'Grizzled Granite and Sons', whose founder Grimley Granite was assaulted by Thud, tore down Thudson's bridge and left him with a bill for demolition services as well.

In retaliation, a rogue tribe of Trolls attacked a Dwarven mining operation in the Black Forest, yesterday morning, and slaughtered the seven long time employees there. This act of agression has led the Dwarven Nation to declare war on all trolls and enact an ordinance requiring all constructions with an outstanding balance owed to be seized immediately and torn down. Dwarven troops have begun to occupy key strategic fortifications as well. They claim that such actions are merely a safety precaution while negotiations are attempted with the Chiefs of the Trolls.

The Chiefs in return have declared war on the Dwarves, and set a bounty of '3 goats for every stupid dwarf squished into sausage!' If there are level heads negotiating a resolution to this situation, they are not in evidence at the present time.

A coalition of mythical creatures has begun to take sides in the altercation, with many species enacting a trade embargo with the Trolls. However, one prominent figure, that notorious criminal known only as The Griffin, has openly agreed to sell either side whatever arms and armors they need to come to a "fair and equitable conclusion".

Unfortunately, now that both sides are being heavily armed, it seems that a swift and peaceful resolution is nothing more than a wishful delusion. -ED

Ingrid & the Painted Dolls

IT SHOULD BE NOTED that personally I don't have much business with monsters and demi-gods, at least not the ones on par with what can be found in the old Greek tales. I try to avoid anything with any sort of real power, as I have found that becoming a pawn in the games of the prominent is ultimately hazardous to my health. So needless to say, if I had known who and what the major players were, I would never have poked my nose into the middle of this particular mess to begin with.

It all started with a bang. Literally. That and an underwhelming tendril of smoke rising from the center of what I had previously taken to be a completely abandoned factory on the outskirts of Detroit. This was not my favorite city, by any consideration, but it did have a plethora of empty apartments to choose from, even some that had working plumbing and no major leaks. I had stumbled into a rather swanky abode, right next door to a sprawling industrial hulk of steel boxes and protruding pipes.

Explosions being in the same category for goblins as auto accidents are to traveling humans, that of a rather irresistible opportunity for spectatorship, I could not help but part the curtains and peer out of the third story window into the factory yard beyond. It was dark outside and snowing, as it was early February and the hour was approaching two in the morning. And though I could not see anything clearly, there was the distinct impression of a commotion. Perhaps my eyes caught the glint of starlight reflected off polished porcelain. Or maybe it was nothing more than an errant dream, winging away to nest itself in a slumbering mind. Both were equally as likely, as you shall see, though I did not recognize the immediate possibility of either. I had to get a closer look.

It was easy enough to find a hole in the fence, around towards the back where some ne'er-do-wells had previously slipped in to practice their artistic skills and salvage copper to cover their rent. This was fortunate, as the barbed wire atop the barrier would certainly have ruined my best flannel pajamas, had I needed to climb over it. Creeping my way through the unplowed snow towards the site of the explosion, I passed derelict cars, crumbling cement walls, piles of refuse, and a mattress. There is always a discarded mattress in places like this, but only the truly desperate would ever think of sleeping on it. Who knows what might dwell among its rusty springs and yellow stains?

While beautiful and surreal under a blanket of white, these trappings confirmed my suspicions. This place was abandoned. Which meant that whatever was happening inside was an illicit affair. If it weren't for the hint of magic in the air, I would have turned around right then and there, for the drug trade holds no promise for me. I like my teeth right where they are.

But this wasn't drugs. Or if it was, there was something that reeked of otherworldly fishiness about it, like an Atlantean tuna or a Grecian mermaid. I had passed at least seven wards of warning and skirted a handful of crude magical alarms. I probably should have given some consideration to the very clear trail of footprints I was leaving behind, but my curiosity was piqued and that made me careless. Maybe if it had not been so cold, I would have noticed the abundance of silken webs glistening with ice and the accompanying multitude of spiders gliding along them like tiny venomous figure skaters. Perhaps that is not the best analogy, but it holds. Have you ever actually seen the terrifying costumes these folks wear? The Olympic Skaters, not the spiders.

I spied a metal door blasted off its hinges. It had been beaten out from within by a rather significant force. The steel was buckled and bent and tossed aside into the snow. Sneaking forward, I inched my face around the frame and peered cautiously inside. The scene within was like the aftermath of a war-zone!

Industrial weaving looms were broken apart and scattered here and there amongst the mangled limbs and severed heads of their rather lovely looking female operators. More wisps of smoke rose from the ruined machines, fire danced cheerfully over the corpse of a large electrical generator, most likely the source of the explosion that had originally drawn my attention, and a greasy sheen of oil spattered the room like an errant spray of blood and gore.

But strangely enough, there was no blood. Not a single drop that I could see. Oil, yes. Fire, yes. Dismembered limbs, undeniably. But no blood. The mouths of the murdered girls, a few possessing heads that were still attached to their bodies, were all open in silent screams of alarm and their gorgeous blue eyes were all wide with shock. But not a single face was distorted in pain, even the ones that were missing necks, and there were no cries of the dying to be heard. Everything was silent, save for the crackling of the fire.

I reached down to pick up one of the decapitated heads by its luxurious blonde curls so that I could examine it more intently. All of the girls that I could see were variations on a single theme, that of dainty perfection. Some had curls, some had bobs, some had blonde hair, and some had auburn. But all of them had rosy painted cheeks that were as cold and hard as ice to the touch, and blue eyes that were nothing more than painted glass with horse hair eyelashes pasted on. No wonder there was no blood—these girls were dolls!

They were nothing more than fancy painted mannequins, all now silent, broken, and still. I had no bloody clue what I had stumbled into, but backing out now was completely out of the question. Things had gone from mildly interesting to downright strange.

I did not have to wait long for the next piece of this surreal winter's tale to fall into place, as the bellow of an enraged fellow broke swiftly through my reverie. "*WHERE IS MY WIFE?*"

A pink fleshy man rumbled into the room. He was size of an elephant, or perhaps even bigger. This giant towered above me, kicking aside the ruined remnants of the faux-female industry with bare feet the size of garbage can lids. Said feet were attached to trunk like legs, if that is, tree trunks had a tendency to drip rolls of bark like this giant monstrosity managed to drip rolls of fat. Thankfully his nether regions were concealed behind a foul stained loincloth made from the scabby skin of an unfortunate goat, with hooves and horns still attached. Falling down over the loincloth was a flabby sagging stomach, and then several more stomachs fell down over that. This all-you-can-eat-buffet nightmare was completed by meaty fists with sausage-like fingers, arms that could pass for ham hocks, man boobs that would have put Dolly

Parton to shame, and a piggish squint eyed face with more chins than a Shar Pei.

Not wanting to be mistaken for his wife, I scuttled backwards as the giant reached down and grabbed one of the painted dolls instead. Stuffing her into his whale-like maw, he chewed merrily away as bits of saliva-drenched porcelain dribbled down his chins and a mohair curl dangled obscenely from his lips. I probably would have escaped without even being seen, had I been focused on where I was going, instead of mesmerized by the beastly glutton before me. And if I had bothered to remember those damned spiders.

A web had been woven across the battered doorway behind me, and I became stuck fast in its sticky lattice. This was no ordinary web either, as the cables involved were easily the thickness of clothesline and as strong as piano wire. I struggled to reach my scissors but only managed to become further entrapped. Out in the snow, I could just make out the towering hulk of the spider that had woven this web, a fearsome thing on par with the giant behind me. No ordinary shoe would ever squash this demonic arachnid. A can of Raid the size of a gasoline truck might not even have done the trick.

For a moment, in my growing panic, I wondered if I had been shrunk down to the size of a doll myself, and if these monsters around me were actually normal size and not the detritus of a Japanese movie that had obviously escaped from the set. My second thought was that the doll girls had very shapely thighs, as I had turned my head just in time to be smacked in the face by one such leg wielded as a club by the corpulent giant. My next thought was nothing at all, since I had been knocked unconscious by the blow.

As should be apparent, since you are reading this book after the fact, I did not die. I was not sucked dry by that monstrous spider, nor ripped limb from limb and devoured by that morbidly obese man-like monster. Instead, I awoke in the dark, tied securely in more of those oversized spider webs, and dangling upside down from the ceiling like a bat. There was absolutely no hope of escape.

Below me I saw, as my eyes adjusted to the gloom and my brain to the angle, a multitude of those life-sized dolls slumped lifelessly against the walls. There were at least another twenty of them, these being whole and unmolested, but they were not engaged in any sort of occupation. Unless the efforts of sleeping can somehow be used to generate commerce. Which of course it can, but I doubted that these creations were simply whores. Stranger things have happened, for sure, but such employment did not explain the sewing machines. Or the monsters.

The dolls were of no use to me in my current state, dangling above their heads on the tangling emissions of a giant man eating spider. Not that I had any proof of its dietary considerations, but a creature that large most likely had no qualms about eating anything that it came across. Except, it seemed, for me. I was still alive, but why? What sort of plans did these villains have in store for me? I did not wish to wait and find out. My arms were tied firmly to my sides, but if I could have reached my scissors, then I might just have been able to do more than cut off my own legs. This seemed to be my only option, so I began to wiggle and squirm in an attempt to loosen my bonds and at the very least free my hands.

As I swung back and forth high in the rafters, the flickering flame of a candle and the illuminated form of a rather plain and frumpy looking middle aged woman appeared below me. She held the candlestick in one hand, and a pot of paint and a pointed brush in the other. She was slightly stooped, with dishwater colored hair, plump features, and archaic peasant's clothes. A kerchief was tied around her head, and a craftsman's apron was tied around her waist. She went to each of the dolls in turn, shined the light on their faces, and painted on their thin black eyebrows with a skillful hand. Looking up at me once her task was complete, she winked conspiratorially and raised a finger to her lips for silence. The warning was quite clear. I stopped my struggling and went limp.

The door below opened once more and the most terrifying sight I have ever witnessed shambled into the room. As I said, I have very little experience with demi-gods, but this was a Nightmare Lord, and there was no mistaking it.

My breath caught in my chest, my heart began to pound, and it was only through the greatest effort of will that I was able to remain still and not scream out in horror. Contrary to the other two monstrosities I had witnessed this one was not a giant, but a man sized thing of spines and jags and razor sharp talons.

Like a poisonous skeletal caterpillar with the face of a man, but with empty bleeding sockets instead of eyes.

"Your fat husband slumbers once more beneath my yoke. His hungry dreams are simmering. Are my weavers ready?" The nightmare thing's voice was the chill wind of the graveyard. He plodded towards the nearest doll and caressed her face with a creepy segmented appendage.

The painter woman gave a curt nod and kept her careful distance from the Lord, risking a glance upwards once his back was turned to ensure that I was still watching. The abomination took a deep breath and sighed forth a swirling putrid miasma - evidently the stuff of dreams, only bad ones. As the fog passed by the face of each slumbering doll, they one by one took a gasping breath and stiffened in turn, rising jerkily to their feet like marionettes seized by the strings. It was truly horrible to watch.

Once all the dolls were animated, via the magical properties of unholy halitosis, the nightmare worm surveyed them with expressionless eyes and softly rumbled, "They no longer sleep, and yet they dream. Put them to work at once. The webs must be woven." Then the caterpillar man turned and shuffled from the room once more.

The dollmaker watched him leave, and waited another minute in silence to make sure he was gone, before snapping her fingers and pointing up at me. The dolls turned towards the sound, alert and awaiting her instructions. "Cut him down. Carefully," she said, and the automatons moved to comply.

They made a ladder of sorts, standing one on the other's shoulders, higher and higher like acrobats ascending to the stars. When the topmost one was finally on my level, she reached out and yanked at the silken strand that held me to the ceiling. It gave way, and I was passed swiftly down the ladder from girl to girl until I stood once more on my own two feet on the floor, still all wrapped up in the spider's web.

The tottering tower of dolls, their task now complete, collapsed like dominoes into a heap. Starting at the bottom of the ladder, one after another simply went limp and was overcome by the weight remaining above her. There was no screaming or panicked flailing of limbs, just an almost orderly dissolution of the structure which left behind an arousing pile of painted ladies with arms and legs akimbo. If my circumstances had been different, I might have considered this to be a personal heaven.

"If you swear to help us, I will set you free." The craftswoman made her way towards me with a tiny pair of seamstress scissors and began to snip away at my bindings.

I glanced back towards the door and quirked a brow in suspicion. "Help you do what exactly? I am no weaver of webs, and I would prefer not to throw my lot in with monsters, as I am sure you will understand."

She shook her head and shivered at the thought of what lay beyond that door. "No, not help them! Help us. Help us escape!"

That I could certainly do. Pretty women in any sort of plight tend to draw my affections, even if they were nothing more than toys given the mockery of life by a nightmare god. I quickly gave my assent and she finished cutting me loose. Already I was hatching a plan, but I needed to know more.

"What exactly are they working on?" I jerked my thumb back towards the door. "I have seen a giant spider, an actual giant, and a Lord of Nightmares. And now you, a woman making dolls. The pieces of this puzzle don't even seem to be from the same bloody box!"

She snapped her fingers and motioned to the only exit. "Stand in the way," she ordered, and the heap of girls sorted themselves out with haste and formed an orderly mass in front of the door to comply. If anyone else came in, they would certainly be slowed down by the wall of dolls standing silently in the way. Once she was satisfied that we would not be discovered, the doll-maker turned to me and sighed with sadness.

"My name is Ingrid, and my husband is the giant, Chahnameed, the Glutton. His hunger is never sated, and too often this means the demise of his bride. But I was clever, I saw what happened to those who wed before me, so I left a doll in my place and he ate that on our wedding night instead. It was the same for every night since, though sometimes I made several extra while he slept, and would venture out for a few days to see the world. That is how I found Inguma. He says he is a bigwig in Basque mythology. But whatever he is, he is crazy and dangerous. Even more so than my husband. I thought he could help me escape, but it was he who captured that giant spider, Tushi-Gumo. And it was he who enslaved my husband in order to harvest his hungry dreams. And it was he who set me to work here, forcing me to make my dolls to weave together the webs of the spider and the dreams of my husband."

"But what are the webs for?" I asked with consternation, still not able to make heads or tails of this whole ordeal.

"To capture and feast on all the good dreams. The innocent dreams of children, the less innocent dreams of young lovers, and the happy remembrances of the elderly. Once there are no more pleasant dreams, no more restful slumbers, Inguma can reign with impunity and move through the hellish dreamscape he has planted, to murder any who dare oppose his rule."

Now it all made sense. Okay, I grant you, not a lot of sense. And there were clearly some holes in this evil plan of theirs big enough to drive a truck though. But at least I understood who the players were and what they thought they were doing. I told Ingrid my plan, and though she was skeptical, she set to work on it right away.

First she painted my face an unblemished ivory, which took several coats to completely obscure my natural copper tone. Then she thickened my lashes, rouged my cheeks, and painted my lips into a delightful red bow. A wig of springy blonde curls was added, and a dress was found that would fit me.

Looking in the mirror, I was amazed by my transformation at the hands of this skilled craftswoman. Sure, I still had my pointed nose and large ears. And while the wig did slightly obscure the later, there was nothing to be done about my rather obvious proboscis. Regardless, I looked hot! If only all goblin women looked this way (heck, if any goblin women looked this way), my world would be a much more loving place indeed.

At the designated time, I lined up with the rest of the girls and we all marched into the sewing room and sat down to work. We did not have to wait long for the Lord of Nightmares to arrive leading the sleepwalking glutton along on an invisible leash. I glanced upward and realized that Tsushi-Gumo was already there as well, lurking in the rafters and spinning out her sticky monstrous threads.

At first, work went on as always. Inguma harvested the dreams of the slumbering glutton in the form of a shimmering silver thread, the spider spun her own silken cords, and the girl-dolls gathered both together then wove them into webs. I handled the cutting, as I had the scissors for the task and not the hands for weaving. If I had touched the webs, I would have been held fast, but not so the unliving girls. They were completely unaffected by the magic they manipulated. Ingrid's husband stirred on occasion, but never completely woke, which gave me a clue how tenuous Inguma's hold on him really was.

I marked the exits. There were two in the traditional sense, the door to the outside that had been blasted through the night before, and the one deeper into the complex through which we had all arrived. There were way too many holes in the roof and the walls however, which meant that we had to keep at the ruse longer than I had anticipated. The work took three whole days and while the dolls did not need to sleep, thankfully the spider did. Ingrid marched her dolls, and me, back to the store room for repairs and respite each evening after the others had left, and we returned each morning before they arrived. As luck would have it, nobody noticed the intruder in their midst during the day. And during the night, I discovered that Ingrid would have made a most excellent bride, if only she had had a better pick of husbands.

Finally, on the third day, the net was big enough and we were ready to spring the trap. I wish I could say that it all went completely according to plan, but these things never actually do.

I had been watching Inguma all morning, being careful to never quite catch his eye. Which was not as difficult as it sounds, since he did not seem to consider the dolls as any sort of threat and barely even glanced our way as it was. When I noticed boredom begin to creep into his face, and the yawns appear on his lips, I took my chance and strode towards the thread issuing from the giant's dreams and clipped it off. This was not out of the ordinary, as it simply indicated that we were finishing a section and needed to start up a new one without fear of entanglements. What was unusual, was the fact that I kept on going, leaned down to the giant's ear, and whispered loudly, "I have found your wife! She is here! Wake up, Chahnameed! Wake up and claim her!"

The Glutton stirred and grumbled, and then sat up rubbing at his eyes. Inguma strode angrily over and swatted me away with his spiny appendages. His face strained with the exertion of his will as he wove his desperate spell and tried to put the giant back to sleep.

"Wake up! See your wife that he keeps from you!" I screamed out as I sailed through the air from the force of the Nightmare Lord's blow. Who knew there could be so much strength in those skinny little caterpillar spines? I had achieved my goal though. I had woken the Glutton.

The giant pushed himself to his feet and bellowed with rage, his eyes blinking open as he reached out and grabbed Inguma in his enormous fist. The caterpillar man was taken by surprise by this attack and squirmed violently in Chanameed's grasp. But even those sharp spines were no match for the Glutton's mindless hunger. The giant raised his thrashing former captor to his mouth and summarily bit the bastard's head clean off. It must not have been the most tasty of treats, because the giant paused for a moment, wrinkled up his flabby face in disgust, and then spit the chewed up remains of Inguma to the floor. He wiped flecks of blood from his lips and belched loudly.

"WHERE IS MY WIFE? WHERE IS SHE?"

As I dashed toward the door, followed by the dolls dragging their enormous net of webs and dreams, the flaw in my own plan became clear. Ingrid stood out. It was clear she was not a doll. She was not even all that pretty. She was a worker and a wife, and she was calling out commands to her creations. "To the roof! Cast the net over the walls! Trap these demons inside!"

The dolls were quick on their feet, even with the weight of the webs slowing them down. I watched them scale the walls of the factory with ease and spread the net over the roof, covering the holes not a moment too soon, as the giant spider was also attempting to escape.

"Run Ingrid!" I shouted, but it was too late. Her husband had spotted her.

He scooped her up with a stupid happy grin on his face and cooed with affection. *"MY WIFE! I HAVE FOUND YOU!"* And then he popped the poor woman into his mouth and chewed merrily away, swallowing her down in one satisfied gulp.

There were no screams from the dying crafts-woman. It has been my sincere hope that she fainted dead away at his touch, and was thus not conscious for such a horrible demise. There was no time then to mourn her sacrifice, though. The netting fell down around the walls, sealing the doors and locking the monsters inside.

I did not remain behind to watch the dolls secure their webbing to the ground. Nor to witness what became of my oversized adversaries. With those two horrors trapped together in the factory room, it was clear to me that they would eventually be overcome by their hungers and only one of them would survive the ensuing battle. Hopefully, which ever one that turned out to be would starve to death shortly after. It wasn't exactly a fair end, but it was fitting. I could not have these creatures' future crimes on my conscious as well, should they manage to escape. There was enough past baggage weighing me down in that regard already.

Over the years, some of the dolls have found me again. Always alone, always silent. They help with the tasks at hand, perhaps as a thank you for freeing them from their servitude to Inguma so long ago. And no, I don't mean to imply any sort of physical relationship. That is none of your damn business anyway. Occasionally one cracks or shatters, or the nightmare magic finally putters out and the doll crumbles lifeless to the floor. But no worries, they are only porcelain and paint after all, and as sure as the sun rises, another eventually finds her way to my door.

✖ ✖ ✖ ✖

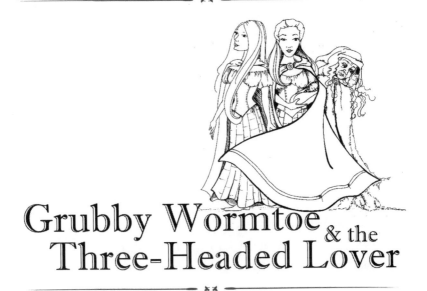

Grubby Wormtoe & the Three-Headed Lover

WOMEN ARE CRAZY. All of them. Every single one.

And while any sane gentleman over the age of twelve knows this fact full well, we don't actually start out pre-programmed with this knowledge. It is a discovery arrived at through trial, error, and experience. In fact, we start out thinking that women are pretty swell. When boys are infants, mothers are their sole means of nourishment and survival. Women are soft, comforting, and soothing, they smell nice and, most importantly, they have the milk!

As boys begin walking and eventually join their brothers in communal education and athletics, girls become gross. They smell fruity, have shrill voices, and they don't like mud. They also tend to run off and tattle when encountering something that is traditionally masculine, such as belching, cow tipping, or grave robbing. Then these boys reach adolescence and everything goes all fuzzy, both on their bodies and in their brains, and they start to think that those icky girls might actually be somewhat swell again. After all, the girls are soft, they smell nice, they have musical voices, and hey—We remember those! Fleshy, bouncy, milk dispensers!

Then comes a few years of awkward fumbling, followed by a few seconds of bliss, and finally the smack upside the head that brings men to their senses and to the inevitable realization that, indeed, all women are crazy! Most of us manage to come quickly to terms with this reality, and see the insanity as an acceptable trade-off for those fleeting moments of ecstasy.

There is also, some speculate, a biological impetus to overlook the madness for the propagation of our respective species. I find that notion, however, to be absolute hogwash, and thus I must dismiss the idea that our attraction and appreciation of the female form is nothing more than a hardwired instinct that forces us to seek your company despite our better wisdom. Most women that I have met aren't so bad after all. In the right light.

My dear friend Grubby Wormtoe, though, had an unfortunate habit of finding those among the female population that are certifiably batshit insane. And that, ladies and gentlemen, is what eventually proved his undoing.

Everyone's had a bad experience with romance, I will grant you that. So you might be thinking that Grubby's problems were just a matter of exaggeration and hyperbole. I counter with the fact that you, I most sincerely hope, have never dated a young lady named Flambodica!

✖ ✖ ✖ ✖

"I have found the girl of my dreams, G!" Grubby blissfully informed me one day. "She is a fire dancer! She gots this skimpy leather top and skirt and these big fans a flamin', and you should see the thrill in her eyes when something starts burning! That's passion, old buddy! And oooh boy, she is an inferno in the sack! This must be love!"

Some of you may be snickering about the idea of a redcap in love. I assure you, it was no laughing matter when she set the bed on fire—actual fire—with both of them in it. Grubby barely made it out with his life. He was all blackened and blistered, and his eyebrows were totally gone. Flambodica was not so lucky. It seems she was rather into trying out kinky new positions and had decided to make up one of her own. This particular position was entitled "The Phoenix."

Not crazy enough for you? Maybe you would find another of his romances more to your liking: Mantista, the bearded lady! Now, perhaps we should not technically count this one, as we had both been drinking that night, and I too missed the signs that it was going to wind up all wrong before the date even started. Let Grubby's experience be a warning to you all, though. When a "woman" has a beard, an Adam's apple, and a bulge in her pants, chances are that the is not just packing a roll of extra socks.

Are you sensing a pattern here, yet? Grubby's ideal match-making site was the fairgrounds, and more specifically, the side show tents. There was the woman who was into some serious bondage fantasies named Arachne. She was under investigation for a string of dead lovers; each of which had been found tied up in her trailer and mysteriously drained of all bodily fluids. He also dated a girl nicknamed Stumpy, a blind chainsaw juggler who was looking for a partner for her new act. And let us not forget Corax, who had an unsettling habit of trying to pluck out people's eyeballs with her teeth.

The point is that Grubby was terribly unlucky in love. But I firmly believe that there is someone for everyone out there somewhere in this crazy messed up world. And then he found her. The one and only. Sort of...

✹ ✹ ✹ ✹

Grubby's perfect woman turned out to be the Gypsy Fortune Teller in a traveling company known as "The Backwater Bacchanalia". They were not a famous troupe, by any means, eking out a living on a circuit that included stops in such prestigious places as Hell-for-Certain, Kentucky; Lizard Lick, Texas;

Hangnail, Arkansas; and Boggy Bayou, Florida. The last one being the home of the "Mullet Festival." Not the hairstyle, but some sort of nasty mud-dwelling fish.

We crossed paths with the "Bacchanalia" in Bloody Springs, Mississippi. Grubby had wanted to visit the town on the name alone. In retrospect, it was probably Fate that steered us there. We had run afoul of her during the 15th century back in Venice, and she had been gunning for revenge ever since.

This fortune teller, a slightly dumpy human woman named Maeve, shared a small colorful vardo with her fifteen year old daughter and her ancient wizened grandmother. She herself was in her early thirties and crowned with long silvery hair. She kept it that way on purpose, as it helped provided a visible aura of wisdom for her act. Her name meant intoxicating, and while I did not see the attraction, she definitely had Grubby under her drunken spell. All things considered, she seemed relatively normal and well adjusted. I should have been much more suspicious.

Though I did not want to begrudge my best friend his happiness, I soon became irritated with his head over heels behavior regarding Miss Maeve. Every morning Grubby woke early to hit the cemetery and snatch some fresh flowers for his love. He attempted to clean up his appearance, which led to a thrift store shopping spree of mismatched coats, velour pants, and plaid socks. And he even took a stab at improving his personal hygiene, if you can call setting off a bug bomb in a gas station bathroom in a misguided attempt to eradicate the long term tenants that resided in his hair much of an improvement.

The worst, however, was his automatic elevation of his new girlfriend to expert status on just about everything. "Maeve says toothpaste is bad for ya, gotta gargle with oil instead." Not that Grubby even owned a toothbrush to begin with, but I am pretty sure that she did not mean motor oil. I said nothing, however, to contradict him.

"Maeve says you gotta leave a bowl of milk out for the pixies at night." We both knew that milk left out did nothing but turn sour and attract stray cats and bugs. Pixies did not often frequent Mississippi anyways, and when they did, they preferred peach liquor and coffee. Again I said nothing, and we soon had a colony of stray cats hanging out at our back door.

"Maeve says murditation will help control my anger issues." This was his explanation when I discovered him naked in the kitchen at three in the morning, twisted like a pretzel with his feet stuck up under his armpits, and a pile of burning air fresheners in a bowl beside him. The pine tree kind you hang from the rear view window of acar.

But he was in love. And he was actually making an effort to be worthy of long term companionship. I bit my tongue, and went on with my affairs. I was determined to let him enjoy being a chained man for as long as it could possibly last. Which, as it turned out, was not to be terribly long. Though surprisingly enough, this was through no fault of his own.

"Maeve is worried," he confided in me one afternoon. "Her cards say trouble is brewing across the realms. Got a conviction coming up, but the goblins didn't send a missionary." He was right... or close enough. The Conjunction was coming, and I had forgotten all about it!

The Conjunction was a gathering of the mythic races that happened once every one thousand years. There would be feasting and fighting and negotiating. It was also required that every mythic realm send forth a human soul as representation. The human's job was to speak honestly of the realm's particular influence in the natural world, and thus hold firm the boundaries and borders. Without an emissary to send to the gathering we would insult the other races, lose our access to the realm of mortals, and ultimately dwindle in power and diminish in stature. It would lead to war and bloodshed, as others rushed in to seize what has deservedly belonged to goblins since the dawn of time.

Maeve was right to be concerned. I sent out inquiries, but received only grim and apathetic replies in return. No, the Goblin Realms were not sending an emissary. A suitable one could not be found. Troubles at home were more important. "War might be good for the economy!" "We will send one next time..." "What do you care, you are banished?" And so on and so forth.

It should be noted that at that time there were only a handful of individuals on the short list to stand as an emissary to the Goblin Realms. They had to have a bit of goblin blood, no matter how far back and diluted it was, and they had to demonstrate that our particular brand of chaos, terror, and madness really did add something of value to the world of man.

From that list of about a dozen souls, most were unfortunately deceased. Goblins, on the whole, make terrible records keepers. Several more were institutionalized, one had found Jesus (and promptly misplaced him again), one was busy with a book signing tour, and the last was undergoing emergency eye surgery and unable to travel. However, I was not going to let this slide without a concerted effort to solve the dilemma. I may have been banished, but that was only a political thing. I was still a goblin and ignoring the Conjunction would be bad for everyone involved, and doubly so for ex-patriates like myself who were already stuck in the middle.

With all this on my mind, I went to visit Maeve and see if her cards could provide any insight or direction. From Grubby's admission, it was clear she was already aware of the problem and was, I hoped, working on possible solutions. She wasn't home, however, when I came calling. Grubby had mentioned something about a shopping trip to an organic farmer's market they had planned for that day.

Her daughter, Nimue, was home though. I found her lounging on a folding beach chair out front of the wagon, with her hair tucked under a large floppy sun hat, a cucumber mud mask plastered to her face, and cotton balls stuck between her freshly painted toes. She peeled the cucumber slices off her eyes as I approached and gave a friendly wave. "Mom and Mr. Wormtoe ain't here. Anything I can help you find?"

"A suitable emissary with goblin blood?" I quipped, frustrated and having no real clue of where to turn for answers. I certainly did not expect a helpful reply. To my surprise, I got one anyways.

"Why not get a child?" Nimue shrugged, as if it were the most obvious thing in the world. "Surely there is some kid out there that would work for you, right? I mean, aren't most kids already born with a goblin mindset anyways, and then society just beats it out of them?"

I was so stunned by the simplicity of this answer that I forgot to even thank her as I turned and raced back to pack my things. I had seen the tell-tale signs of a goblin-touched babe in the birth announcements of the local hospital. Therefore, I had a pretty strong hunch where we could find such a child. I figured Grubby would have to miss out on this particular adventure, but he was at the campsite waiting for me when I retured.

"You seen Maeve today? We was 'sposed to go shopping."

I hurriedly explained my plan to him, and to my surprise he heaved a sigh of relief and flashed his horrible oil stained smile. "Hells yeah! Let's do it, G! I hate shopping!"

And so we "borrowed" a car and set off to the Baptist Memorial Hospital without delay. We had a solution. It was so simple. Nothing could possibly go wrong!

✷ ✷ ✷ ✷

I never cease to amaze myself with how mistaken I can actually be. Evidently, there is a widespread paranoia about security in your modern society. It seems that when the fae folk abandoned the practice of stealing children, not everyone got the memo. And indeed, there are many mortal idiots who have stepped in to fill the hole left in the market by our departure. Often, perhaps, their motivation is not monetary, but a delusional sense of their own parenting abilities. As if stealing someone else's baby makes any sort of positive statement about one's suitability to shape and nurture a young child of their own. Granted, we were about to do just that, but for a really good reason!

It was much easier back when childbirth was done at home, and all we had to do was trade out a new born baby for an animated sack of twigs and potatoes. People tended to be less observant in those situations. Instead they were elatedly drained after the ordeal and overjoyed by the fact that they had just successfully accomplished what every other animal before them had also been able to do, namely squeeze out an offspring without exploding. Many forgot to bar the doors and windows with iron, wrap the baby in clothes turned inside out, and place an open pair of scissors in the crib.

Of course nowadays, nobody puts scissors in a baby's crib, unless they fancy a visit from child services. Instead, hospitals have security guards, coded doors, and miniature house arrest alarms that are strapped to the child's ankle moments after leaving the womb. The first two were not a problem to the likes of us; a little booze, a little glamoury, and a scuttle through the air vents were stock in trade for our adventures. The last one, however, was slightly more difficult to surmount.

✖ ✖ ✖ ✖

"Nope. It is stuck on there good, G. This danged thing ain't coming off!"

Grubby and I were in the NIC unit beside our chosen emissary's crib. To protect the innocent, we will call him John. This works for the narrative because that is what his parents had already named him anyways. Let's at least hope he had a really impressive middle name, like Kingslayer or Tarantino. (He didn't. It was Dalton.)

John had entered the world a few days past and was under observation on account of him being born early, according to the standardized testing modern human children are now subjected to beginning at conception. Thankfully the nurses had been able to convince his father to go home and shower and sleep for a bit. It would have been much more difficult for us to steal the child out from under the nose of both of his parents.

Grubby and I tried everything to get that damned alarm bracelet off. Even oiling the poor baby up like a greased pig with a stolen bottle of Vaseline. But still, it would not slide off. There must have been some sort of special key involved, but we did not have the time to hunt through the ward in order to find it.

Instead, Grubby finally decided that we should just saw the leg off and let the kid start an early life as a pirate. In desperation, I agreed. Though as the barber amongst the two of us, I insisted on being the one to actually perform the surgery. Grubby pulled out his sack of strange and random things and rummaged through it. He emerged with the spindle of an old piano stool, to serve as the boy's new leg, and a rusty saw for the procedure itself. I aquired a staple gun from the supply closet to secure the peg leg back on.

We drew a dotted line with a marker just above the baby's knee, as we had seen this done on surgery shows on TV. Grubby held the leg still on either side of the line and I laid the saw against the soft pink flesh of this newborn child. Taking a deep breath, and focusing on the task at hand I pushed down and was suddenly brought to my senses by a cry of alarm.

"What are you doing to my baby?" I turned to see a young woman in a hospital gown, thin and wasting away, with sunken hollow cheeks and the spectre of death reflected in her eyes.

"Damnit, Grubby! What were you thinking?" I admonished my friend. "You put the mark in the wrong place! Don't you even know what a circumcision is?" I shrugged and tossed the saw into the trash can. The gig was clearly up, and we had botched this entire operation.

"The distance 'round the outside of a circle?" Grubby murmured in slow confusion. "What's that got to do with anything, G? And don't you worry none, miss. We already gots lots of nice happy band-aids all ready." To prove his point, he began to stick the small yellow smiley face strips all over the infant's body.

"Are you friends of my husband?" The woman sank down into a large reclining chair beside the crib closed her eyes, and tried to catch her breath. She was clearly not well. And then it struck me. This child did not have just any old insignificant drops of goblin blood, it had trow blood. Very fresh, and very strong. This was the babe of a Kunal-Trow, which meant that his mother was the human wife of a Kunal-Trow. Which meant that she was fated to die for giving birth to such a child. And she probably knew it too.

As gently as I could, I told her of the predicament at hand and about the need for a goblin blooded emissary. She in turn demanded that we leave the room so she could hold her baby in peace and quiet. We both stepped outside the curtain and debated in hushed voices whether we should hunt for a new child or just hit the woman over the head, grab this one, and run. A few moments later, before we had the chance to reach an agreement, the mother interrupted us again.

She was standing in the doorway of the room and holding her newborn son along with a tiny teddy bear. There were tears in her eyes as she held the child out to Grubby, and then the teddy bear out to me. "It's a funny thing about these bracelets, you know. The babies seem to get them off with no trouble at all." She tickled the sole of her son's foot, and indeed, he squirmed a bit in his sleep and managed to slide that blasted alarm right off.

I snatched it from the air before it hit the floor, stuck it around the teddy bear's leg, and tossed the stuffed toy into the crib. That would do for a stand in until we could return the child in a few days' time. "He will be safe with us, I promise you that. And we will bring him back as soon as we can."

The mother nodded and slumped back down into her chair. "I know you will. He is going to be a great man someday, my John. His grandfather was a soldier, but he will be a peace maker. Already his destiny calls to him. Go and do what needs to be done. Make my baby a hero. I'll buy you the time to slip away..." And then she closed her eyes and breathed her last breath.

Somewhere down the hall, an alarm went off. The woman must have been wearing a monitor for her vitals as well. As the nurses came running in, we slipped into the shadows and then waltzed right out the front door amidst all the confusion. John slept soundly through the whole thing.

✻ ✻ ✻ ✻

We reached our stolen car with the baby, but found it surrounded by a gang of pugnacious urban pixies. They were drinking from a bottle of Southern Comfort, not milk, and seemed to be itching for a fight. The light of the streetlamps glinted off their switchblades and brass knuckles as they advanced upon us sneering and slinging threats.

"Give us the baby, boyos!"
"Yeh can't take him anywhere."
"End of the road, suckers!"

Some people are born to be politicians. Some are born to be musicians. Grubby was born to make a mess, usually out of other folks' faces. He tossed the baby over to me and charged forward into the fray.

Blows were struck, bones were snapped, and blood sprayed forth in perfect imitation of those dancing fountains at Las Vegas casinos. Grubby was winning of course. He was a redcap and only the drunk, dumb, or suicidal would pick a fight willingly with a creature such as he. So why had a gang of thin and breakable pixies been sent to steal back the baby we had already rightfully stolen? The whole situation reeked of poor planning and desperation, unless—

"Grubby!" I shouted as realization struck me. "It's a stall tactic. They are buying time for the trow to return!"

Technically, if you go back far enough, Goblins and Trolls are of the same bloodline, like different branches of an old diseased tree. But there was little love lost between our respective species. The blood in the child would serve well enough for our purposes at the Conjunction, but an actual confrontation with an angry trow would go ill for us. It was time to cut and run.

The car was a lost cause, marked as it was now by the belligerent pixies, and I was barred from using the traditional faerie roads, due to an old disagreement with an oaken elf lord. Those would have been the easiest route across the country, but they were also the ones most likely to draw further attention upon us. Public transportation was right out, as there was no way I was hopping on an airplane with a newborn, at least not without ear protection. The Goblin Roads would be too suspect, and if you want to be picky about it, I wasn't supposed to use those either since my banishment. Which left only one reliable option, The Ways of the Dead.

There was most likely a cemetery close by, seeing as how hospitals and churches often go hand in hand. But we had something even better at our disposal, the morgue. With luck, there would even be a fresh corpse to use as our ticket onward.

I whistled to Grubby and dashed back inside the hospital. He followed after, battered and covered in pixie blood. They wisely chose not to pursue us as we were headed back inside, which is pretty much where they wanted us to be, trapped and waiting for the trow to return and discover our crimes. We hopped in the elevator and I pressed the button for the basement. Grubby grinned jovially at the other passengers, a timid elderly couple, and explained his frightful appearance away with a shrug.

"Car accident." The couple nodded nervously, and edged back into the corner of the elevator. "Dey was accidently in the way of my car, so I pummeled dem. Lost a tooth too. Wanna see?" Then he opened his enormous maw to show off his new battle scar with pride.

Thankfully, the elevator dinged before he could continue this conversation, and the door opened up onto our floor. If the ride was much longer then we probably would have had two more corpses on our hands, but we really only needed the one. Old people can be so fragile, and Grubby's face was enough to frighten even the stoutest heart into skipping a beat.

I had been banking on using the kunal-trow's wife as our passport, but she was not to be found. I had no idea how long they let a dead body sit upstairs for the loved ones to say goodbye, but it would probably be there at least until her husband came back. We did not want to still be around when that happened.

Instead, I laid the baby down on a cart of body bags for safe keeping, while Grubby opened the lockers and checked the toe tags for the freshest body we could find. My dim-witted companion whistled in amazement after the third or fourth examination. "Dat must have been some party, G. All dees folks is naked!"

"And yet, not a single one is fresh enough!" I exclaimed in exasperation. We needed a body not more than a few hours past its expiration date and unfortunately all of these corpses were from yesterday. It had evidently been a surprisingly unsuccessful evening for this hospital.

Though it pains me to admit it, Grubby's quick thinking is what saved us. Or perhaps it was just his keen nose. His thick brow furrowed and he snuffled at the air with a perplexed expression, looking for all the world like a Chinese pug trying to root out a peculiar scent. He held up a finger to forestall my impatient questioning, and began to wander around the room, sniffing at the lockers, the tables, and even in the trash cans. Finally he stopped before a heating vent, ripped it off its hinges without hesitation, and reached in to withdraw a freshly dead pigeon. "Somebody musta been saving 'em for der lunch. Freshly dead. Twenty minutes at da most."

It was the best we had, so it would have to do. I retrieved the baby and together we retreated to a hidden vantage point behind the mortuary door. Grubby stood in the center of the room holding aloft the dead pigeon. Once he was ready I placed a bone flute against my lips and blew a raspy and almost inaudible note.

Almost instantly the floor began to shake and the walls began to rumble. The locker doors banged back and forth on their hinges and a ghastly fog coalesced around our feet. A bloodcurdling train whistle shattered the sterile serenity of this temporary tomb. It was a noise loud enough to wake the dead. The spectral steam engine screeched to a stop amid a spray of sparks that flew from its invisible rails, and it came to rest right beside Grubby and his pigeon. We had successfully summoned her from the cold beyond, Charon's modern day ferry for the souls of the dead, *The Bone Orchard Belle*.

The conductor stepped out, a shriveled sunken skeleton of a man in a dusty moth eaten black uniform. He pursed his toothless lips at Grubby and scowled with irritation. "What's this? We do not stop for poultry! Who will answer for this summons? Who will pay the price for falsely calling on our service? You..." A bony finger stretched out to poke Grubby in the chest. "Shall I take your soul instead?"

"Dis ain't poultry, ya bone head! Dis here is the Emperor of TimBukTu..." Grubby nodded knowingly at the dead bird and then added by way of explanation, "Turned into a pigeon." He held up his other hand and counted as high as he could on his fingers. "One... two... three... thousand years ago by a rotten witch. Kicked the bucket in the end, and he gots as much right to ride this train to his bolivian as any other sucker on der! You just tell me dat he don't..." Grubby balled up his fist and grimaced at the conductor, daring the poor withered man to call his bluff.

Thankfully, he didn't. He merely quirked a brow, plucked the pigeon from Grubby's hand and sighed the sigh of a long suffering civil servant. "We shall be duly honored to escort the soul of his Imperial Majesty to his final resting place, or point of reintegration, once the records are consulted and his wishes, beliefs, and previous conduct made clear." The conductor scowled once more, stepped back up into the carriage, and slammed the door in Grubby's face.

The whistle blew, the fog churned, and the train began to chug forward. As it quickly built up speed, I stepped from behind the door and took up position next to Grubby. The floor shook, the walls rumbled, and at the last possible second Grubby's arms shot out. One hand snatched me up by the back of my vest as I clung tightly to the trow-blooded child while the other one snagged the railing of the caboose as it thundered by. There was a sinking sensation, the howl of a chill wind whipping around us, and then a sharp clatter of pain in the knees as we tumbled onboard our chosen cross-country transportation. The hard part was over. Now we could ride on in peace.

✖ ✖ ✖ ✖

Normally we would have climbed under the cars and secured ourselves there in the rods like the train hopping hobos of old, with the dust in our faces and the sights rolling by on either side. I felt that it was unwise to subject the baby to such an experience, and of course there was the risk of him tumbling off and being tossed into some random underworld or hell. I could just see us trying to explain that one to the trow.

"So we stole your kid, watched your wife die, hopped a train through the underworld, and unfortunately lost the boy in Mictlan... But hey, don't worry. I am sure a four year journey through horrible soul crushing desert terrain will be a piece of cake for such a strong willed and well prepared baby."

We took up residence inside the last car instead, travelling as common tourists for the sake of our package. I had heard many enticing things about the *Bone Orchard Belle*, from the plush velvet cushions and the crystal chandeliers that sparkled with the light of the heavens, to the extravagant feasts of exotic foods and the painted virgin harlots to attend to your every need. That last one always stumped me though, what good is an inexperienced harlot to anyone? We saw none of these varied delights, however. Clearly, this was a coach class car.

The seats were well worn wooden planks and the rusty walls were plastered with ancient faded posters and public service announcements:

SAFETY!
Is no longer our concern...

THE NATIONAL RECYCLING COALITION
Thanks you for signing the organ donor card

DEATH AND TAXES ARE INEVITABLE
Late Fees May Still Apply

The floor was covered with dirt and a few rotten twists of yarn from the original carpet runner, and th only light in the entire carriage came from a single flickering bulb that swayed back and forth on its bare wire cord. As bad as the accommodations were, the passengers were worse. Like the New York City subway in the predawn hours, everyone onboard looked rumpled, washed out, and exhausted. Their eyes were glazed over in an impassive blank stare, their mouths drooped at the corners, and occasionally one would sniff or sigh without ever making eye contact with anyone else. Even when the trow baby started to cry, nobody looked our way.

"Something's wrong," I whispered to Grubby. "Why is he crying? Did you drop him on his head again?"

Grubby shrugged and tried making silly faces at the child to cheer him up. This only made the boy cry harder. Understandable of course, as Grubby's normal face is enough to bring most folks to tears.

"Maybe he is hungry..." I ventured. "What do babies eat?"

"I gots some bad whiskey? Will dat work?"

"It is possible. It will certainly put him to sleep. We should give it a try!" And so, we gave the baby whiskey. It was just a few shots, but clearly the child could not hold his liquor. It all came back up in a sticky mess spattered across Grubby's shirt and pants.

A loudspeaker crackled and a distant muffled voice called out, "Next stop, Yellow Springs. All passengers departing for Yellow Springs, please have your tickets stamped and ready." Nobody in our car moved. The baby continued to cry.

"Dis ain't workin G. Imma go call Maeve. She gots kids. She knows what ta do." I rolled my eyes as Grubby headed off to find a pay phone on the train.

He came back after a few minutes to borrow a dime and then departed again to make his call. I wasn't sure how such a thing was supposed to work here, or who the dead were supposed to contact. Maybe it was a way for them to say one last goodbye, if they had remembered to bring spare change. Calling collect was probably frowned upon.

"She is on her way," Grubby declared smugly as he sat back down on the bench beside us.

"How is that even possible? It is a train for the dead. Oh crap! Is she going to kill herself? Bad plan, Grubby! Really bad plan!"

"Nah. Don't worry. She's a witch. She'll find a way."

And indeed she did. Not twenty minutes later the door to the next carriage up opened and Maeve sauntered through. She was dressed in her best funeral finery, a black dress with lots of lace, a black pillbox hat with a single white flower stuck in the band, and a raven perched on her shoulder. Ravens were both psychopomps and witchs' familiars, so of course she had a ready guide with which to find us. She smiled warmly to Grubby and nodded politely to me as she took the baby from my arms and then gave a disapproving frown. "Why, this child is soaking wet! He needs to be changed."

"That's probably from da whiskey. And we can't change 'em, we ain't got another to trade him for."

Grubby received from Maeve a stern, scolding glare for his honest explanation, which was followed by a swift whack upside his head. She then tutted softly to the child and ushered him away to be changed and fed. Probably from one of those delicious feasting cars we had heard so much about. Grubby and I remained behind in purgatory.

When Maeve returned a few hours later, she discovered quite a different scene in our train car. Grubby had grown bored of the tedious quiet in the car and had somehow managed, after much growling, grunting, and a few well-placed sucker punches, to get our formerly morose traveling associates to participate in a rousing sing along. The whiskey had been passed from soul to soul as we belted out, the ladies first and then the men, the words to an old bawdy drinking song.

> *"Who's that knocking at my door?*
> *Who's that knocking at my door?*
> *Who's that knocking at my door?"*
> *said the fair Young Maiden.*

> *"It's me and my crew*
> *and we've come for a screw!"*
> *said Barnacle Bill the Sailor.*

> *"It's me and my crew*
> *and we've come for a screw!"*
> *said Barnacle Bill the Sailor.*

"Will you take me to the dance?
Will you take me to the dance?
Will you take me to the dance?"
said the fair Young Maiden.

"To Hell with the dance!
Now off with your pants!"
said Barnacle Bill the Sailor.

"To Hell with the dance!
Now off with your pants!"
said Barnacle Bill the Sailor.

There was laughter and mirth, drinking and song, as life once more flourished amongst the dead. Well, maybe not life, but perhaps a kind of warmth. Memories and hope flowed back into those poor lost souls, and the glazed looks slowly faded from their eyes.

The loudspeaker crackled to life again, "Next stop, Flowerland. All departing passengers, please have your tickets stamped and out for inspection." The crowd, almost as one, looked wistfully towards the doors and visibly deflated. They had no tickets to stamp. That was why they were stuck back here.

But we could not dwell on the sadness of others. We had our own plight to deal with, and Maeve had returned with a fearful look in her eyes. She handed the babe back to me and whispered harshly, "You have to get off, now! Grandmother has caught wind of your exploits and she is coming to take back the child! Hurry up and go!"

I had hoped to ride the train all the way to our destination in Oregon, but California would have to do. It is true that we had managed to dodge all of our enemies so far - the trow, the pixies, the security guards at the hospital. But the deck was stacking up against us and I did not fancy facing off against a withered hag as well. I waved to Grubby, tossed the baby to him, and flung open the back door. We were going to have to make a jump for it.

Again, Grubby's intuition, or perhaps it was just his gregarious nature, managed to save us. As I stood there with the door open, he bellowed to the rest of the passengers in our car. "Dis is your chance folks! Everybody off!" He barreled out the door and leapt off the back of the train, landing squarely on his own two feet atop the tracks. To my surprise the others began to follow suit and lept off the back of the train after him. Now granted, none of them landed quite as well as he, but it was not like they could break their necks in the fall or anything. Finally it was just me and Maeve left in the car, and I turned to see if she was coming with us.

A startling change had come over Grubby's girlfriend. She had let down her long silver hair and it flowed wildly out around her skull. Her posture had become stooped, her hands twisted into arthritic claws, and her face was now bitter and cruel. In a rage, she tore at her fine clothes, ripping them away from her body and leaving her standing there in nothing but an ancient tattered shift. She looked then, for all the world like an old angry hag and I did not dally for explanations. My survival instincts took over and I leapt with Maeve's "grandmother" hot on my heels.

Dashing towards Grubby and the baby, I managed to gasp out a warning, "Wicked Witch! Run! Head north!" He glanced over my shoulder to see the horrible old lady running after us and took off at a fair clip into the woods. We were surrounded by huge trees, as the ancient and venerable redwoods of Northern California rose up all around us. I had never had the chance to visit them before and they practically hummed with ancient songs and powerful magic. It was not the time for sightseeing, though, and I followed swiftly on behind Grubby.

Here is where our liberation by Grubby's actions becomes clear. By encouraging everyone else to jump out as well, he had created the perfect wandering mass of confused people. They were shambling around on the tracks, much like stunned cattle, and generally getting in the way of our pissed off pursuer. It gave us a pretty good head start and slowed the grandmother down considerably, as she cursed and screamed at the shades of the dead to get out of her way.

Unfortunately, the old places in the world that were full of natural magic like this proved more of a boon to the witch than to us. Grubby was at home on the battlefields and moors, and I have always been a domesticated sort and therefore not entirely comfortable out in the middle of a forest. What lead we had gained was quickly lost once the crone broke free of the milling mob and came howling after us.

Grubby tossed the baby back to me and turned around to face the oncoming storm. Confident that he could handle anything this old bat tossed at him, I continued on, though my pace slowed and I glanced over my shoulder to make certain of his success.

"Why ya chasin us, Circe? We ain't done nothin wrong!" Grubby held up his hands and called out to the witch. This gesture of peace did him no good, as a second later he was ducking the lightning bolt that flew past his head. It crashed into one of the ancient trees behind him, blasting the venerable wood to splintery bits.

"You may have tricked my granddaughter, but you cannot trick me! Give back the child that you have stolen! He shall not be a treat at your feast!" Spittle flew from the enraged hag's mouth and her hands reared back to toss another spell.

"Whoa, crazy lady! You gots it all wrong! We ain't gonna eat da kid. We just takin em to the consumption." This was perhaps the worst mispronunciation Grubby could have managed at that particular moment.

The wicked witch howled in fury and slung her spell. "Quiet! Foul swine!" The focused magic hit Grubby full in the chest and sent him tumbling backwards, head over heels into the leaf litter. I stopped in astonishment and turned back to draw my wand. I was no match for this witch, of that I was certain, but she had just killed my best friend and I was not going to let that stand unanswered.

As I stood there, the baby in one hand and my wand in the other, a curious scene unfolded before my eyes. Grubby had not been blasted to smithereens. He had been hit, that is for certain, and it most likely hurt like hell. But he was still there, rising to his feet once more. The issue was, that he now had four feet to rise on. And a snout. And a curly little tail. Grubby had been turned into a pig.

Upon seeing the transformation that her spell had wrought, the witch's hands relaxed from their claws. Her stoop disappeared and she stood up straighter. Her hair even seemed to come under control and fall down in silver waves once more around her shoulders. Finally, her face softened and lost its withered crone-like qualities. Tears began to pour down her cheeks and Maeve, as she was clearly Maeve once more, sank to her knees beside Grubby and began to wail.

I turned away and journeyed onward, leaving the woman to her grief. Grubby was fine. Well technically, Grubby was swine. But he wasn't in danger of being killed any time soon. I still had a job to do and this baby needed to be delivered to the Conjunction. Grubby's sacrifice would not be in vain.

✖ ✖ ✖ ✖

By early evening, I had joined the gathering in the hills of southern Oregon. There a huge bonfire had been laid, and around it danced enchanted mortals and mythic folks of all persuasions. I gave the baby over to some wild men, half fae all dressed in colorful pirate garb, and they took him into the dance with them, making him the head of their goblin parade. I wandered away from the fire and sought out a stiff drink. I found solace in the form of moonshined absinthe and I drowned my troubles deeply in its bittersweet depths.

The babe was returned to me at dawn, this time by a gaggle of smiling gnomes. "You did well, Goblin." They spoke in satisfied tones, but I ignored them in my drunken stupor. "This child will stand for goblinkind, his whole life long. He has sung highly of you, and your violent friend. He has told of the bravery and sacrifice of two stupid goblins. Of a journey through the land of the dead, of the cleverness and heart you have shown, and he has at last danced with all of the mythic souls. You have done quite well indeed. Now, farewell, till our paths cross again."

❧ ❧ ❧ ❧

The journey home was uneventful. I deposited the babe in his crib once more, beside his grieving father, and removed the teddy bear imposter I had left behind. Having a trow for a dad would not be the easiest upbringing in the world, but I knew that this child now had protectors and friends of every sort watching out for his well-being. I was sure I would see him again someday.

I made my way back to Mississippi. I am not quite sure why, but I had a feeling that I would find Grubby there as well. I did, but he was still in the form of a pig.

He was snuffling around the front yard of the vardo, with Nimue lounging in her chair beside him. Well, she might call herself Nimue, but now that I knew what to look for, it was all pretty clear. Her silver hair was done up in pigtails, her makeup applied in a childish overdone manner, and her baggy clothes obscuring her rather more mature and motherly body. It was only Maeve dressed like, and in the mind of, a child. The old crone had been her as well.

The girl looked up at me and smiled. "Grandma Circe is awful sorry about what she did. She figures it is time to retire now, since she is getting more easily confused these days. Mama is downright pissed, but she isn't ready to be a crone yet, and I am sure not ready to be a mother. So we gotta wait a bit till I am."

I nodded, even though I did not understand, but said nothing in reply. Instead I just watched Grubby for a while as he foraged in the dirt.

"He's gonna be okay with us," Nimue said. "We will take care of him, I promise. And we are all vegetarians, so it is not like he is going to get turned into bacon one day. I am glad things worked out with the baby. Are you gonna hang around for a while? Mom thinks you're kinda handsome, after all."

I shook my head and walked away. I had no room in my life for a pet pig right then, and no spell to turn him back. Though if one existed out there, I would find it. He was safe among those women... woman... whatever. But I knew that I would not be. Crazy women and I never really work out well in the end. And like I said at the begining, all women are crazy. Of course, all the men are too.

The Last Meeting of the Homeless Hearth Society

"**GOBLONIAN SHIT STORM!** Read 'em and weep boys..." I laid down the complete spread, man, pot, and fire, followed by wind and lightning. Beating such an excellent hand was possible, but certainly unlikely, especially in a game of five card stud.

"Watch your language, Mr. Gandersnitch! There are ladies present!"

The protester was Mrs. McBunion. She was a meddling busybody of a woman, but we tolerated her mostly because she was the one who organized the monthly meeting and secured the parlor at the private gentleman's club where we secretly gathered. It was good for our sorts to be among humans, especially humans from the old families that still possessed both wealth and power. The fact that the club had overnight lodgings for its members was an added bonus as well. It was a lifeline for most of our gathering, as it was the only thing some of them had to keep them going. Thankfully, the club itself had fallen on hard economic times and was open to renting out space, on occasion, to particularly esteemed non-members, such as our Mrs. McBunion.

Now, I don't want you to get the wrong idea about our benefactor. Certainly, she was old. I would wager that she was technically even older than I am, but it is never polite to bring up the topic of a lady's age. The problem was she acted old. Her mothering, nanny-goat, prim and proper behavior was not just an affectation. It was as much a part of her as was the severe school marm's bun of her weathered grey hair and those horrible clunky black shoes she insisted on wearing. Her mannerisms were as ingrained in her being as were the sparse silver hairs ingrown into her chin. She saw us, the members of the Homeless Hearth Society, as her charges. Of course she did. She was a Glaistig, a supernatural Scottish nanny.

We were all household spirits of one stripe or another, each of us displaced and cast adrift. McBunion was the only one of us still attached to a reliable home of sorts, and only if you counted the Southgate House for the Elderly and Infirm as a reliable sort of home. It was certainly a far cry from the generations of blue blooded children she had reared in her prime. The fact that her former family had petered out into a gaggle of boozers, drug addicts, and pedophiles, the entire lot of them dead or behind bars, should not be seen as a reflection on her. She had protected them through childhood, as was her duty, and had been truly devastated when there were no more offspring in the offing and the family mansion had to be sold at auction in order to pay for mounting court costs. Still, she managed to hang on, and was reaching out to help others do the same.

"Bah! Blow it out your zhopa, you old goat!" McBunion's almost exact opposite, the thimble headed Mohra, placed her cards face down on the table and took another swig of her vodka on the rocks. A fold.

Mohra was a hard worker and used to rough living, having followed a family of Russian immigrants to America during the 1930s. She was as thin as a bundle of sticks, with an abusurdly small head bobbing atop her bent body. Her hands were wrinkled and pruny from years of washing and scrubbing, but she was as dirty and grubby as McBunion was clean. I found it highly amusing that her existence revolved around helping others with their cleaning and yet she herself was never unsoiled. She was a formidable card player, however, and a professional drinker. I had lost my shirt to her many times before in our games of Hog-swallow. It was purely by chance that I was ahead at all.

Mohra's situation was complicated. Her downfall had started with the invention of the flushing indoor toilet. Then there was the electric washing machine, the electric vacuum cleaner, the dishwasher, the dryer, the electric iron, and the microwave oven. The abundance of electric sewing machines revived her spirit for a time in the seventies, but the influx of cheaply made garments soon dashed her to the gutters again. She had been overly optimistic about a new after-shower soap scum spray, as that might get people back into house work again, but it did not pan out quite that way. We had tried to help her set up her own cleaning service once, but she kept breaking into her customers' apartments in the middle of the night and scolding the hard working career women for their slovenly ways.

Therein is what I brought to the group. No, not my slovenly ways. I tend to be quite tidy, when it matters. It was my ability to think outside the roles traditionally assigned to us and my skill at working the system that I had been thrust into that kept me alive and well without a household to claim as my own. Technically, I am a homeless hobgoblin. But I have managed to craft a convincing replica for purpose out of a stubborn insistence of focus. And that is what I was attempting to teach my fellow hearth spirits in similar predicaments.

Take for instance, the next player at our table, Kaspar. He was a kobold who had worked merrily away in the coal mines of Pennsylvania. His tapping had warned the miners of dangers, he had dragged them out of harm's way when they dug too deep, and he had pocketed a nice little pension from the bits of precious metal that they carelessly discarded. But even his diligence couldn't keep up with the greed that drove the company boss, and a horrible disaster finally shut the whole thing down. In the shadows under his eyes, you could still see the last breaths of those trapped miners. He had stayed with them till the end, but he could do nothing to save them. He only managed to sleep anymore due to the copious amount of rumplemintz he drank.

"Deine Oma masturbiert im stehen! You cheating little hob! Where are you hiding the extra cards? In that fancy vest of yours, I'll wager!" Kaspar wasn't one to trust anyone anymore, especially those with the appearance of wealth.

He had taking to hanging out with the human homeless, haunting the stairs leading to subway stations and sitting atop sewer grates. I was hoping we could one day coax him back down under the ground, but that was a long way off. He leaned back in his chair and glared at me as he tossed his own cards away as well.

"Get your boots off the table! You are getting dirt everywhere!" McBunion swatted at his shoes as she passed by with a cloth napkin and then dropped it, with averted eyes, into the lap of the one we called Grue. He had used his own napkin to cover the chair, in an effort to be more civilized. McBunion had almost fainted with worry about the upholstery when she had realized, at our previous gathering, that Grue wore no pants.

He did not, as a point of fact, wear any clothes at all. It was a matter of pride that he didn't really need them, as he was covered from head to toe with hair. You could still make out that he was male, especially when he became excited, and you could tell his backside from his face with a little bit of effort. The face had ears sticking off it and was the part at the top.

Grue pushed the hair out of his eyes with one hand, and grinned mischievously as he made the napkin in his lap rise to a peak. We all knew this was just an attempt to get a reaction out of the old marm, and it worked. She flitted away from the card table, fanning herself and muttering about the improprieties of the lower class.

Really, that was the whole of the Grugach's issue. It was no longer acceptable to have a small, shaggy naked man hanging around the property, even if he was an insanely strong and dedicated worker. "What the Neighbors Might Think" had become more important than cultural identity and folkloric traditions. There is also the fact that children are more coddled in modern times and one might accidentally spot the naked chap going about his day. As a result, uncomfortable questions could emerge such as, "If he doesn't have to wear clothes, then why do I?"

And so, Grue's old Irish master, after a rather heated argument with his new American wife and a night spent sleeping in the motorcar, had one day presented him with a uniform. Which meant, unfortunately, that Grue could no longer be of service to them. His continuing need to go au-natural had, of course, precluded any further opportunities for employment. I actually had no clue how he was managing from day to day. Speculation was that he had taken up residence in the local dog pound, masquerading as a common mutt. I personally suspected that a job in the underground adult film industry was much closer to the mark.

Grue peered at his cards, then over at mine, and back again once more at his own. He then laid them down slowly, one by one. Woman, Water, Fish, Fort, Crown—Crap! He had played a Priestess of Poseidon. He might have had me beaten, but it fell to the two of us to debate the merits of our particular hands.

"What's that supposed to be, Grue?" I asked, playing the fool. "Some sort of mermaid? Mermaid King of the Castle... Wet lady eats royal fish at home? That doesn't even make any bloody sense! You've got nothing." I knew what he had, and he knew what he had, but I have never admitted to being one who plays fair.

Grue did not answer. He just shook his head and tapped his cards on the table, glaring at me. Grue never spoke. Which gave him a rather distinct disadvantage in a game where you have to defend the righteousness of your own position. A game where bluffing, bluster, and bullshit is all part of the process.

"I'm sorry Grue. I don't see it. Clearly you think that you have something, but nobody knows what it is. We all know what I have though. Just look at it. Fiery, greasy dung everywhere! Red hot, butt clenching, eye watering diarrhea coursing through your body like a hurricane! Think of the pain! Think of the stench! Think of the children! You say a soggy tart and her dinner beats that?" I slammed my fist down on the table in defiance. "Not bloody likely."

Grue gave a deep sigh and shrugged, pushing his cards toward the center and relenting. Hogswallow just wasn't his game. Granted, we were being very lenient by allowing him to pay his ante in bottle caps and buttons while the rest of us dealt in actual coins. The real point was to socialize and have a good time, not to actually screw each other over.

In a leather wingback chair by the fireplace, Old Tom snorted and sat upright. I thought he was going to challenge me and come to Grue's defense. Which, while outside of the provenance of the game, would have forced me to reverse my claim and give the hand over to the Grugach. Nobody crossed Old Tom, not even me. There is an ingrained esteem that age affords, and Tom was, as far as anyone knew, the eldest among us all. We figured he had been around when the first humans crept out of the trees in the Black Forest and took to hiding in caves. He was the original house spirit, even before the Romans came along and bound the old ones up into little shrines.

However old he was, his fiddle had not been bowed in many, many years. I had never known him to be attached to a household, and it seemed he simply coasted by on the memory of whatever honors had been bestowed upon him in those prehistoric times. To my relief, he did not rise to scold me. He simply yawned, stretched, and fell back into a restful slumber in his warm and cozy chair, with his dragon-cat curled up at his feet. His meal stayed untouched on his lap, as his ancient teeth most likely could not have handled any of it, save the potatoes and gravy.

But the plate was there as a sign of our compassion and respect. And as is the case with most things, it was the thought of it all that really counted.

The hand was assuredly mine, though there was still one player left to fold. I shrugged sheepishly at him and gave a dastardly grin before reaching towards the pot to rake it in. He quirked a brow and grinned back, holding up a single finger of warning to delay my triumph.

Mr. Piccadilly was his name, and his story was perhaps the saddest of them all. He was a Boggart, a brownie gone bad. He was like an unlucky penny and nearly as impossible to get rid of. He had actually been housed at Parliament of all places, which was as posh a posting as us hearth folk can get. But over the years, it had become political suicide to express a belief in the old ways. It made the MPs seem simple and common if they gave any credence to folk tales.

And so, little by little, Mr. Piccadilly had changed. It was subtle at first, his teeth had grown sharper and he had developed a tendency to cackle loudly in the wee hours of the morning. His "issues" had culminated in fits of books being flung about, windows shattered, and compromising pictures leaked to the press. Ultimately several priests and TV specialists had been brought in to cleanse the place of ill humors and lingering shades. He had been forced to pack up and take to the road, haunting hotels and hostels as he went. I actually liked him better this way, dangerous and aloof. But my fondness quickly soured as he summoned up that horrible cackle of his and tossed his cards down with a flourish, face up. Fire—five times over. A complete hand full of it, and placed there most unfairly by fate.

"Sign of the Devil, old chap! Unlucky for you, but how fitting for me. Up in smoke, burn it all down! Anarchy reigns supreme!" He pulled his winnings into a pile in front of him and rose to his feet. "Back in a bit. Gotta check on the rodent."

The rodent in question was an oversized South American thing, rather incorporeal and only mildly self-aware. It was more than an animal but less than person, and had a rather nasty habit of drinking the drool that fell from the mouths of slumbering humans in the homes it chose to inhabit. Still, as a hearth spirit of a sort, it was as welcome among us as Old Tom's dragon cat was, so long as someone took responsibility for it; which Mr. Piccadilly had done. He always seemed to have an interest in helping the underdog out, at least until it became apparent that there was nothing in it for him. Then his apprentice was usually dropped like a sack of moldy potatoes.

"Bloody well done! Fierce game, so? Mind if I sit in for a hand or three?" Butler flopped down in Mr. Piccadilly's abandoned chair and held out a bottle of excellent Irish whiskey. His selection only made sense seeing as how he himself was Irish and quite at home in the cellars. I had earlier assumed that he was simply late to the party, but the reality was that he had been exploring the club's stores in order to select the choicest bottles for our enjoyment.

The whiskey was passed around, glasses filled, and a toast eagerly declared by Kaspar. "Ein Prosit! To the health of all, except for Schweinehund Gandersnitch."

Butler's fall from grace had come during the prohibition years. The cellars he inhabited had been raided, the bottles confiscated, and the contents emptied into the street. He had holed up in Chicago for a time, consorting with gangsters and gin runners. But he wasn't a criminal anymore, just a connoisseur. The recent resurgence of niche wineries, craft brewers, and small label distillers gave him the freedom to pick and choose his haunts. Once again he was a satisfied soul, and truth be told, an even snappier dresser than myself.

The last of our gathering was Boris, the Domovoi. He was the closest in appearance to an actual bogeyman, with an overly large head and a thick bushy beard. A dark streak existed in him as well, a survival tactic if you will. It was common amongst his sort to besiege the nearby Domovoye in an eternal rivalry of neighborhood one upsmanship. They protected their chosen family while attempting to make things more difficult for the families around them. And if there had been some sort of insult or injury committed against their own household, they became even more vigilant and aggressive towards their peers.

It was also customary for a Domovoi to move with the family when the need to relocate arose. The problem was that Boris had been more fond of his actual house than of the family that lived there. So when they moved, he tried to stay behind. The new Domovoi moving in had discovered him hiding in the attic, beaten him soundly, and kicked him out into the cold. Boris, displaced, disgraced, and disgruntled, tracked down the family that had betrayed him, and summarily smothered them all in their sleep.

"I do not understand this game you play. Too much talking. Too much lying. Next, we play chess, da?" Nobody was going to play chess with Boris. Frankly, he scared us.

It was Morha's turn to deal next, and she chose to play it safe with a simple discard dilly-down. She played a card with the symbol for air, Kaspar trumped her with wood, Butler tossed away the heart, I took control with fire, and Grue ultimately got his revenge with water. We played on like this for a few hours, nobody ever really gaining control. Just being in each other's company was victory enough.

Mrs. McBunion puttered aimlessly about and eventually sat down for a snoozeworthy game of dominoes with Boris. Old Tom continued to snore in his chair, while Butler kept us slightly inebriated, and Morha entertained us with her dirty jokes. We laughed, we played, and we bonded over shared troubles and fond memories. For a while there, we felt almost like family. We were rested, rejuvenated, and connected, as each of us desperately needed to be.

As the evening began to wind down, Mrs. McBunion looked up from her game with a perplexed frown. "Has anyone seen Mr. Piccadilly lately? He has been gone an awfully long time. I do hope he is alright."

I shook my head. Nobody had seen him since he won that round, and that had been hours ago.
Grue sniffed curiously at the air, catching a scent that the others could not quite smell. We all felt it though. Something terrible was about to happen. Old Tom sat suddenly upright, a look of alarm in his crusty cataract-veiled eyes. Then we all smelled it. Smoke! The Club was on fire!

Alarms sounded, much too late, as all around us the carpets smoldered and the walls began to blaze. Thick black smoke stung our eyes and stabbed at our lungs. I grabbed McBunion's hand and led her down the passageway, hacking for fresh air. Boris and Morha stumbled out close behind, supporting a singed Grue between them. The reek of his burnt hair was enough to make a person sick. Butler ran out weeping and clutching the whiskey bottles close to his chest. Kaspar had been right beside him, but turned back for Old Tom. Neither of them made it out of there.

As the old club crumbled, so too did our company. The last thread of hope and home for Boris, Morha, and Grue burned to ash and blew away. One by one, they too faded into dust.

The rest of us could not even bear to look at each other. Our friends were gone, and there was nothing we could do about it. We still had our lives, as strained as they might be, and we shuffled back to them again in silent mourning.

We never met after that. How could we? Each of us knew that all we would hear, and all we would see, would be the memory of Mr. Piccadilly's horrible cackling laughter as he stood there in the flames holding a can of gasoline. And a match.

Otterbourne

THERE STILL EXISTS, among the fae and mortal alike, the persistent perception that I am bitter, cruel, and remorseless. In short, a womanizing cad. And while three out of five ain't bad, I must protest that painting my persona with such a broad brush will never reveal the nuances and details of my life. There is certainly a swath of shadows to my history, but there are also many subtle points of light. As you have seen, I simply reside between the lines. I am a balancing act, liable to tip to either side on a whim. I am not evil. I am not good. I simply am.

It is also a widely held belief that by our very nature, our hard wired physiometry as it were, goblins are incapable of crying. This is patently false! I submit as proof the fact that in my lifetime I have shed one single tear. That may not be much, but it was enough. It was a tear shed for a woman.

My most unfortunate tale took place ages ago, back when I was still on the run and hiding out in the hills and forests of the New World. I was trespassing on the lands of one of the many minor Oak Kings who populate the globe, secure in the knowledge that he was too busy to notice me. He was locked in a war with the Catoctin Trolls, and had been for as long as anyone could remember. Besides, I did not think he was the sort to hand me over to bounty hunters for a paltry reward.

This mountainous landscape was peppered with all sorts of pathways to other mythical realms, both natural and faerie made. Pockets of old magic still lingered in many of the caves and hollows, though who left them there remains a mystery to this day. The end result was a sort of labyrinth that I could navigate easily and escape from quickly, should the need arise. I did not, however, take into consideration the enmity of the squirrels whose home I had unwittingly invaded.

As a hobgoblin, I prefer the comforts of a civilized house; a roof, a bed, and a hearth. In a pinch, a tent will do, if it must. So I considered myself quite lucky to have stumbled upon an abandoned, yet only slightly rusty, silver airstream trailer in a secluded little hollow of the forest. It was in need of a serious scrubbing, so I raked away the leaves from the roof and removed plenty of rubbish and rot from inside. I also chased away a family of squirrels who had been nesting therein, confident that they would find a more suitable home amongst the trees.

Evidently, the squirrels took offense at this eviction and decided to protest my occupation with vigorous displeasure. They began an unrelenting barrage of scolding, acorn pelting, and sabotage raids upon my food stores. They even left little squirrel droppings in my breakfast cereals.

One of the smaller bandits discovered my canister of non-dairy creamer, which I only kept around for its marvelous flammable properties as I don't even drink coffee. This squirrel chewed a hole through the bottom and spread the powdery substance, like a clumsy crack addict, all through my besieged camp. Indeed, powdered creamer must have had some sort of stimulant effect on the woodland rodents, because they kept returning to that canister throughout the day, clearly strung out and trying to get their fix.

Based on what happened next, the only logical assumption I can come to is that those squirrels were all higher than a damned kite. They suddenly ceased their harrying tactics and went straight for a full on bodily assault. One charged in and bit me on the ankle, and a second latched onto my tail. While I was cursing heartily and trying to dislodge my attackers, I reached for my wand so that I might blast them into smithereens.

This was a mistake. As I lifted my head in triumph, the third squirrel leapt from a tree, landed on my face, ripped off my spectacles, and darted off into the woods with them. As quickly as they had attacked, the other two suddenly disengaged as well, and took off after their compatriot. Their mission had been accomplished. I was pissed off and functionally blind.

I followed after, tucking my wand away. It was useless now, as I couldn't see well enough to hit anything with my magic. I could not even see the path before me, and relied instead on the squirrels' chittering laughter in order to follow their trail. I stumbled over roots and rocks, was smacked repeatedly in the face with low hanging branches, and sunk up to my knees more than once in quagmires of putrid mud. When I finally caught up to those rotten little rodents, I was battered, disheveled, and enraged.

I was also standing in the center of a ring of mushrooms. Even I did not need my glasses to recognize the tingle of faerie magic that surged through my body as it yanked me through the veil. The air smelled older and cleaner, and the weather was warmer even though twilight had surreptitiously descended.

I was about to hop right back through the ring, not wanting to be discovered with cold iron in a land that would not look kindly on my presence. But then I heard the sweet singing of a female voice. All thoughts of retreat vanished, and I inched my way forward in an attempt to spy the source of this beautiful music.

The unseen lady was singing a strange old song in the language of the elves. I don't speak elvish very well, but even without knowing the words the song was hauntingly beautiful yet rather defiant sounding all the same. It was a Scottish battle hymn, I was later to learn, and the only sort of song she knew, a product of her upbringing in the Oak King's court of strife and glory. Roughly translated, the words went something like this:

"The deer runs wild on hill and dale,
The birds fly wild from tree to tree;
But there is neither bread nor kale
To feed my soul and me."

Suddenly her song ended and was replaced by an anguished cry. Echoing through the hills, her call tugged at my heartstrings like a siren's song pulls at the breaths of sailors. This clearly sounded like trouble; but despite my better judgment, I was entranced. I had to find the source of this voice even if it meant risking my neck to do so. And find her I did.

She was standing in the center of a ring of stoic Drus, the male dryad soldiers under the command of the local Oak King. They had no weapons drawn, at least none that I could see. But let's face it, all I could really see were blurry tree-things with arms and legs advancing towards a vague slender green form with a reddish smear at the top. That slender form was waving a torch of sizzling fire back at them in futile self-defense.

She was outnumbered, and clearly on the losing end of this skirmish. As I have a soft spot for the underdogs in any situation, and was already snared by the magic of her voice, I foolishly leapt to her aid. My eyes were worthess, so my magic would have to do.

Now, goblin magic is usually dark, dangerous, and powerful, even if it is often completely unreliable. Hobgoblin magic is rather more reliable, yet much less impressive. I could not summon beasts or bones to join our efforts, nor could I blind our foes, or rip out their wooden hearts with but a word. Being of wood though, I could perhaps bind them together into a more useful domestic shape. Shoes and brooms were right out, buckets and ladders would have been less than useful in this situation, but perhaps a fence would be the ticket!

With my wand held out like an assassin's knife, I rapped the nearest Drus in the back of what I hoped to be his head, and whispered my word of command. It was not a complete nor instantaneous trans-formation, as Goblin magic is lessened within the realms of the more courtly faeries. But the tree-man I had struck jerked suddenly in surprise, his feet plunged deep into the earth, and his arms reached straight out to each side as he grasped onto his adjacent peers in a panic. The spell rippled through each soldier as they were grabbed in turn, each stiffening and reaching out as well to form a quite effective, and thankfully immobile, sort of living fence.

Of course, I had also trapped the woman inside said fence. This proved of little challenge to her, as she stepped up to one of the incapacitated tree-men and set her torch to his outstretched arm. In short order his unfortunately rigid appendage was alight, and moments later nothing but charred ash remained, with a softly smoldering stump where his elbow had once been. The waif gave a little shrug and stepped through the gap.

"I believe these are yours, Goblin?" she asked in a teasing, impish tone, and held forth my spectacles.

"Why, yes... Uhmm... I... Thank you, miss." I fumbled for my words and slid the glasses on my nose. What sort of faerie confusion was this? What sort of trap had I sprung? How had she claimed my stolen spectacles, and why was she being assaulted by the Oak King's men, and how—how could anyone look so amazingly lovely? My heart skipped a beat as my bespectacled vision now became clear.

This is not so much a metaphor, one's heart skipping a beat. It is an actual medical fact, signifying a minor heart attack in a moment of extreme shock or surprise. Akin to having the wind knocked out of you, or your breath stolen away, it is a dangerous situation to find oneself in. Like that moment of climax when the mind goes blank and you realize that you could very easily expire right then and there, if your body did not fall back on long held patterns of proper biological operation. It almost always does, of course, return to the automatic and routine. But the real danger is that in that moment, you wouldn't care if you did actually perish. My entire world had suddenly changed.

The nymph that stood before me now, the one that I had heard from afar, sought out, and rescued, was unlike any lady I had met before or have ever encountered since. She wasn't like those airbrushed sexual icons on the covers of mortal magazines. She was the real deal, slender and athletic with long supple limbs, though she stood shorter than me by hands length at least. Elven sorts are often much taller than I, though it is true I have grown a bit in both stature and girth since leaving my native realms.

Her eyes were a bright sparkling green, which matched the color of her well fitted tunic and breeches, and all of her clothes were embellished with subtle copper trims. These were the Oak King's colors. She carried no torch, as I had first assumed, but sheltered a glowing ball of flame that danced in the palm of her hand. A short untamed mop of russet colored hair crowned her head like a flickering fire, and a spray of freckles scattered like burning embers on her sun kissed skin. This living embodiment of the forest's beauty was consummated by her thin pointed ears, pert pixie nose, and the subtle whorling patterns on her flesh, reminiscent of the knots and rings of trees.

I have always had a thing for pointed ears, and here I was smitten to my very core. Certainly a departure from the hags and harlots that haunt the goblin realms, she was an elven soul with the bearing of an oak, the spirit of a fire, and the vivaciousness of a satyr. She was also totally out of my league.

Silent for what seemed like an eternity, watching me with a mischievous grin, a smirk to melt even the coldest of hearts, she finally replied. "No... Thank you, goblin, for hearing my call and rescuing me. It is customary in these parts to reward such bravery with a lady's favor." She winked and her green eyes sparkled merrily as her hips shifted to tantalize me.

She was teasing me and I knew it well. I recognize the games women play to get their way and I have, for most of my existence, been a master at playing right along. But here I felt that I must tread carefully with this one, or I might just lose my wits. I forced myself to remember that I was a wanted man, and that there was nowhere I would be truly safe.

I nodded a warning towards the circle of Drus. They were shaking off the effects of my spell now that the circle had been broken. Or technically burned. We did not have much time to linger in conversation.

"I beg no favor, maiden. I did what any gentleman would have done, when stumbling upon such an uneven fight. And such an exquisite sight. Perhaps, so that I might know the shade that will forever now haunt my dreams, you might grace me with nothing more than your name?"

"So you say, silly goblin. But you could not see me, just my plight." Her smile slipped as she passed the ball of flame from hand to hand in contemplation and then finally shook her head tentatively, as if sorry to disappoint me. "Alas, names have power, Mr. Gandersnitch. I cannot give you mine, but I shall instead grace you with a kiss."

And indeed, before I was able to respond to the shock of her already knowing my name (which in retrospect, of course she would have, as my wanted posters were everywhere), she rose on her tiptoes and planted a sweet kiss at the corner of my mouth. Then with a parting glance back at the stirring soldiers, she turned and darted off into the forest once more.

I stood there, stunned and confused, but also acutely aware of the danger I would be in once those tree-men fully recovered. I started back to the mushroom ring muttering out loud to myself in frustration. "Well shit. You blew that one, didn't you? The most gorgeous girl you have ever met kissed you, and now you will never see her again."

I was so lost in my own despairing thoughts, that I did not at first hear the siren song of her voice rising over the hills again. There was magic in her song, most assuredly, as if she were aware of my ill spoken words. But it would not have mattered to me, even had her song had been totally mundane. I was snared, and how.

"Yet I will stay at Otterbourne,
Where you shall welcome be;
And come ye not at three day's end,
A false lord, I'll call thee."

Her words were a challenge, an invitation. And I'll be damned if I didn't accept it. I was not a woodsman then, nor am I now. If it weren't for goblin magic and skillful friends, I would never even have a campfire crackling. But I set off without a thought, wandering the twisting landscapes of faerie for my elusive prey. And she teased me along with laughter and song from the hollows and secret ways.

Around the edges of battle fields I chased her, never too close to the action, but close enough to be of service to those fallen treefolk or suffering trolls that had been wounded and left to die. Even banished as I was, I still had a job to do when I could. Outcast or not, I was still a barber.

I mended those I found that could be mended, and mercifully extinguished those that I could not. I bandaged the blasted and burned branches of the tree-men, or skillfully cut away limbs that were too far gone to be saved. I removed poisoned splinters from trolls, or stitched up bloody jagged holes left behind by barbed Drus arrows. I held the hands of the dying as they passed on, and listened silently to tales of their loved ones left behind. I even removed a spear from the eye of a troll sergeant. It was a tricky operation, as one false move might pierce his brain. The eye of course could not be saved, but he still sends me a thank you card once a year, and tells me stories of his great-great grandchildren.

On the third day of my slow but steady chase, the wind shifted. The thunder of cannons echoed off the rocks and blasted in my ears, and the smoke roiled in to obscure the way. I was suddenly in the thick of the war, with fighting and dying all around me.

As I said before, this conflict was many ages old and had started over a long forgotten territorial disagreement. It was in full swing before the Europeans arrived to plunder the riches of the Americas, and is still being waged to this very day. I have purposefully been sparse with details and clues as to my exact location during this time, as I don't want some addle brained mortal seeking out evidence of this conflict. It would not end well for anyone involved. You should also bear in mind that the things of myth and faerie often exist outside of mortal perception anyways, moving in their own ways, and in their own time frame. You might simply see a fallen tree, and not realize that it is actually a dying soldier from this ancient war. All the better for you, really. The immortal moans of mythic corpses are not a terribly pleasant sound.

The Catoctin had surprised their foes with a skillful flanking maneuver, which the Drus were now desperately trying to repel. Heavy artillery had been rolled in behind the front line of trollish berserkers, and the fiery doom they belched forth was laying waste to copse after copse of the treefolk. That was until a squad of Drus cavalry arrived, assisted by a handful of mercenary centaurs. Arrows and spears and cannon fire blocked out the sky, and one errant shot even came perilously close to ending my own life. It hit the troll sneaking up behind me instead.

While the Drus do rot away slowly as they die, trolls thankfully simply turn back to stone when they expire. There is no mess to clean up at all. You just have to pray that you aren't beneath one when it succumbs. Once they have perished, however, they can make an excellent hiding place; and so I dove beneath the petrified casualty with the arrow in his throat for cover.

The ground shook and the smoke stung my eyes, but worst of all, the beckoning song of my elusive siren had fallen silent. I craved the sounds of her voice as much as I yearned for a second kiss. Eventually the tide shifted again, and the battle moved away. The smoke cleared and the hills stood still. I cautiously ventured forth only to find myself encircled by a ring of wood and steel. The Oak King's men had me surrounded once again.

They marched me deep into the forest, away from the battlefront, while I cursed the treachery of women and my own foolish eagerness to follow along with her games the entire way. My wand and my scissors were taken from me, and I was not about to try to escape my escort without them. I had no delusions of defeating these well trained soldiers without weapons, and no desire to leave my belongings behind should I slip free. I was brought roughly to the royal hall, which was really just a clearing ringed with ancient trees and a throne at its center. There sat the gnarled and venerable Oak King of these lands. I fell to my knees in suplication before him, but only because I was pushed from behind.

The centuries of war with the Trolls had left this particular king scarred and slightly stooped, as if his shoulders bore an impossible weight. His skin was aged bark, his limbs were thick and powerful, and his gaze was distant and cold.

"My men found you hiding on the battlefield. I presume you are a spy. But for whom? What is your name? What is your business?" His deep, slow voice reverberated through the clearing.

He did not then know who I was, much to my relief. "I am not a spy, great lord, and I have no business in your battles, not on either side. I am just a traveler, passing through, and seeking something lost to me."

The king stared unblinking at me, and then tilted his head and thrummed deeply as a trio of squirrels scampered down from the trees and climbed up his rugged torso to chitter in his ear. They were my squirrels! Well, the ones I had displaced. The ones I had chased. The ones with the dairy creamer addiction. What were they doing here?

"A goblin that tells the truth... of a sort. How novel," the king rumbled forth, and I said nothing at all to contradict him. "My vassals tell me of your crimes against them." He gestured both to the one armed Drus I had maimed in our first encounter and back to the squirrels that I now realized were evidently his spies. I was pretty much screwed at that point, and I knew it.

"But I also hear that you have been lurking on the fringes of the battle fields, and healing my tree-men. Healing our enemies as well. So say again, you have no business here? What is it you claim to have lost?" The king glared at me with an upturned brow, silently demanding that I answer his question.

"A woman. A damned witchy manipulative woman, alright? A stunning red haired waif who tricked me and led me on a wild goose chase straight into your midst. Seriously, I am chasing a god damned woman. I don't care one whit about your crazy war!" I was agitated by the appearance of the squirrels and let all illusion of courtly decorum slide.

To my surprise, this brought forth a snort of laughter from the Oak King, followed by a deep groan. "It would seem that you have found my daughter. This bodes ill for you, goblin. Many have had their hearts snared by her smile, yet none have ever caught hers in return."

"Your daughter?" I asked in confusion. She did have a dryad quality to her, but there was something more. Something not entirely of this world.

"Aye. Emberly." He sighed the sigh of a long-suffering father, but now at least I knew her name. "I was foolish in my youth, and spread my seed both far and wide. My children number many, but she is the one that vexes me the most. Her mother was of the stars. A goddess of fire and flight, a comet that passes this way only once a millennium. We lay together but a single night, though that was enough. The next time she ventured near, she left behind the girl. To grow and learn among us, as the stars are too lonely a place for a child."

The daughter of an Oak King and a comet? That was a strange thing indeed. Still, there are stranger things in heaven and earth, and it did make an odd sort of sense. The situation I had found her in, however, did not.

"I came to her aid when she was besieged by what I believe to be your own men, Oak King. This seems rather odd. What sort of father sends soldiers to torment his own child?"

"You know nothing of what you speak!" The Oak King bellowed at me as he slammed his fist into his throne. The entire grove shuddered in response. "A king does what he must for all of his people. What sort of father am I? The sort that can not control the wild whims of his daughter! She ventures too far, she is willful, and she disobeys my wishes. She cannot be still, but she must be made to obey the ways of my realm! We are at war, and I cannot let her selfish nature give the enemy an advantage. My people will suffer because of her fancy!"

I opened my mouth to retort, but the king cut me off with a wave of his hand. "Leave these hills and forget my daughter! My soldiers will find her again, they will subdue her, and her will shall be bent to serve mine. Within the season, she will be married off to the Mox, and we will once more have the advantage against those damned trolls! Begone, goblin! You are not welcome here and my daughter is not for the likes of you."

I was escorted back to the borders of the Oak King's lands, and only then were my possessions returned to me. The warning was clear. If I crossed the boundary again, then my life would be forfeit. But now that I had seen her and saved her once, how could I abandon the girl to the ill fate chosen by her warlord father?

Her name coursed over and over again through my brain. Her bright face floated in my mind. Her kiss still lingered on my lips. Emberly... Emberly... Emberly... Truly, names did have power! And hers had etched its spell on my heart.

I returned to my camper, free for the moment from the harassment of those crazed squirrels, and I began to pack my belongings for the journey onwards. I was restless though, torn between my desire to rescue the beloved waif and the need to ensure my own survival. I laid down to sleep, determined to finish packing in the morning, put her from my mind, and be on my way. But I could not sleep. Still her name kept me awake. Emberly... Emberly... Emberly...

It was no use! I leapt from my bed, strapped on my scissors, and set out into the night. I would find this girl and save her if I could. I would give her the opportunity to flee alongside me, or to remain behind with her oppressive father and ultimately become the wife of the Mox. Once I knew her wishes, then I could form a plan of escape. Or, if need be, wash my hands of the whole affair.

> *"But go you up to Otterbourne,*
> *And, wait there days of three,*
> *And, if I come not ere three days end,*
> *A false knight call ye me."*

Her song reached my ears as soon as I stepped through the mushroom ring, as if it were a message left in waiting for my return. Clearly I was to go somewhere and wait for her, but I had no blasted clue what the Otterbourne might be. Otters live in rivers, so I had been told, but where were they born? In an underwater nest hatched like furry fish from eggs? Don't laugh, biology is not my strong suit and it made sense at the time.

Thankfully I was saved from what promised to be an ill-fated and soggy search of the riverbanks by a well-timed falling star. The Oak King had said that Emberly's mother was a shooting star and in the faerie realms there is no such thing as a simple coincidence. Everything has a hidden meaning. You can almost choke on the layers and levels of symbolism in the most mundane of occurrences. This was a pretty blatant sign, and thus I followed it.

The star led me to the top of a rocky outcropping, almost a minor mountain, deep within the troll's territory on the faerie side of the veil. Was this her Otterbourne, a secluded peak covered in heather and open to the sky? I imagined that it was, and pictured her lying here at night on a blanket of leaves as she searched the heavens for a glimpse of her mother passing by.

I settled in to wait for this girl that I hardly knew, and tried to plan what I would say. Not to mention attempting to figure out what the hell I was doing there at all. My adjournment was not long, and certainly not the three days indicated by her song.

Within a few hours, she had crept up the side of the hill and stood facing me with an encouraging smile in her eyes. She held the sphere of flame cupped in both of her hands, which lit only her fingers and her face, like a child playing games with a flashlight in the dark. And whether simply a trick of the light she held or a reflection of the warmth I felt rising through my bones at the mere sight of her, she seemed to radiate an absolutely angelic glow.

"You came," she whispered, clearly pleased at my presence. "You came back for me, you who can be so horrible and cruel." She wasn't teasing now, nor was she chastising. She was simply stating the facts. I could be horrible and cruel.

"Your father means to trade you away for an advantage in his war. I may not be noble, I may not be kind, and dammit all, I am probably only completely bespelled. But I have fallen head over heels for you, Emberly, and I can't stand by and let that happen. Unless you do want to marry..." I did not dare say the name of her betrothed, but braced myself instead for the impending rejection of my own unspoken suit. I expected the laughter of astonishment and perhaps a bit of noble pity. Maybe she wanted to be the wife of the Mox, maybe she did not. But there was no way she would ever yearn to be mine.

"The Mox?" She wrinkled her nose and frowned in disgust, while I mentally berated myself for causing her smile to falter again. "He is a giant toad that controls the mushroom rings. He is a powerful creature indeed. But I shall not be his wife. I would rather die than become his Lampad bride and wander his nasty underground realm. It is you that have my name, and with it, my heart."

"Thou shalt not yield to lord nor loon,
Nor yet shalt thou yield to me;
But yield thee to the braken-bush,
That grows upon yon lily lee."

Her mesmerizing voice rose softly in song once more, and she touched the flame to her hair, where it caught and began to weave its way across her brow. I stepped forward, thinking that she meant to immolate herself to avoid the union, and cried out in alarm. "No! You don't have to die. You can come with me!"

But the flames in her hair seemed to cause not even the slightest amount of harm. She simply smiled and stepped forward, placing her hands around my waist and resting her chin against my chest. Uncertain of how to proceed, and wary of scorching my nose, I gulped down a protest and wrapped my arms around her as well. It was the most comforting gesture I could muster. This had never exactly been my forte.

Not another word was said as she lifted her gaze, beamed at me, and placed another sweet kiss on my lips. It was not my nose that was burned but my ear, just a bit, from the tilt of our heads bringing flesh to flame. I did not mind it in the least. She pulled away, and taking my hand, she guided me back down the cliffs to the forested realm below.

Now, as I explained before, I am not one to kiss and tell. Though, technically that is exactly what I have been doing. What I mean to say is that I am not writing smut, so you don't get all the intimate details here to drool over. We touched, we kissed, and our souls entwined. Okay, whatever. That sounds terrible. I totally got laid, and it was the purest, most magical, and most completely intimate experience of my entire existence.

Afterwards we walked through the night, hand in hand, pausing every so often to steal another kiss and share another sigh of contentment. And as we gazed into each other's eyes, and sunk down once more in each other's arms to the forest floor, another eternity of bliss. I no longer expected treachery, nor cared if it would in fact be the end result of this tryst. I had never felt a night of peaceful wandering such as this, my fingers intertwined with those of the lady I loved, and I am certain that I never shall again.

We came at last, in the wee hours before the rising of the sun, to the mushroom ring once more. Lying in wait for us were the Oak King and his men. Their blades were drawn, their faces stern and remorseless, but still I drew my wand to fight them. Emberly simply shook her head, and held me back.

"She cannot go with you, Gandersnitch," the Oak King intoned, his voice giving rustle to the leaves on the trees. "Your return has been for naught. Your trespasses, however, shall not go unpunished again."

"I may not best you, you heartless wooden tyrant, but I shall stall you long enough for my love to flee. Of that, you can be most certain." He knew my name now, which was terribly problematic, but I was not deterred. Still Emberly held me back, gently but with all the force a fire has to keep one's hands at bay.

"He speaks true, my love," she murmured. "I cannot survive in the world of man, my flames will falter and die. And you are banished from your own lands, so we can seek no safety there. I grant you now safe passage from my father's realm. That is all that I can do. You have my name, and thus my heart. But I have lived too long among the trees. It is here, my love, that sadly we must part."

I tried to protest, to declare that I would find a safe place for us both, though I knew such a fancy to be impossible. As I have already said, I was smitten, and those in love never are able to think things clearly through. I had no time left to dissuade her, for my words were cut off with one last kiss.

She slipped slowly from my arms, her promise of safe passage keeping her father and his Drus at bay. A wry smile crossed her lips and she raised her hands towards the sky, lifting her voice in song one last time.

> *"The Otterbourne's a bonnie burn;*
> *'Tis pleasant there to be;*
> *But there is naught at Otterbourne*
> *To 'fend my soul and me."*

The fire from her hair spread down her neck and over her face. It crawled up her arms and spread over every inch of her body, engulfing her winsome form in living flame. My earlier fears were made true before my very eyes. The tunic of her father's court smoldered away to ash, and her feet left the ground as she began to rise with the heat of her own inferno. As we stood there, all of us men rapt and helpless, she became no more than a streak of fire and took to the sky to rejoin her mother.

A single tear fell from my eye and landed atop a mushroom of the ring. As warm as the night with Emberly had been, my heart was now stone cold with loss and despair. I did not hear the Oak King as he cursed my name and barred me from ever using the mushroom roads again. I did not see his troupe turn away, bereft of the advantage they had sought to gain. I did not even dare breathe, till the light of my love had faded away into the dark morning sky. Too far away to follow, too far away to see.

I finally glanced down, as the sun rose, and saw that my tear had frozen in a perfect drop around that tiny mushroom where it fell. I plucked it up and, for the last time ever, stepped out through a faerie ring and back to the realm of man. Emberly had granted me safe passage, so the portal allowed me my escape. But the Oak King's word also has sway, and I have been unable to walk them ever since.

I still hear her name in my head, taste her kiss on my lips, and see her glowing smile in my dreams. So believe me when I say thus. Anyone who claims that a goblin cannot cry is both a liar and a fool.

I cried once. I still carry the proof.

☙ ✘ ✘ ✘ ✘ ❧

Strange Company

AT A CROSSROADS IN THE WOODS, just off
the beaten trail, there is a fire.
Ringed with stones and strange faces.
A beacon in the night.
A gathering point at the end of the day, before we
journey off on our separate ways.

The ambassador slumps in his chair, softly dozing
with a bottle on his lap; his old friend Jim.
To smudge the edges into sleep, soothe away the itches
of nature's wards, and ease his aching bones.
We don't ask him for a story, though he tells them
anyway.

Not the ones the mortals hear,
But stories of his life and friends and strange
  wanderings.
To other friends, at other fires, there might be stories
  told of us.
These aren't lessons to be learned,tricks to be
  marveled at, or political points of view to be
  debated.

They're just him.
His expression of self, told through tales.

No one mentions the changes we see.
The tail that wasn't there before.
The one ear gone pointed.
It wouldn't be polite.
He knows well the dangers of walking the line
  between the worlds of myth and man.

I gave him a hag stone, last we met.
Two holes.
One for looking in on the faeries, and one for them
  looking back at you.
Maybe this wasn't wise.
He draws enough attention as it is.

With a stump as a stool, the young green one strums
  her uke.
Softly she sings her silly songs of snowmen and coffee.
She so desperately yearns to be pretty.

To blend in.
Wings, and flowers, and tutus.
I understand, I have a thing for pointed ears as well.
Though the wings just get in the way, if you know
      what I mean.

She hasn't yet realized that she already is beautiful.
What else can it be, when children want to grow up to
      be her?
So she plays the fool, and chases foolish dreams.
Nobody tells her to stop though.
We all want to see her catch them.

Her constant companion snores from the underbrush.
Not the cockroach. The jolly green giant.
Loyal, faithful, loud when he laughs, and good at
      hauling stuff.
What more could a one wish for in a man?
Sure he breaks things...
Often.
Big deal.

It is a by-product of his enthusiasm.
And his gigantic hands.
Mine to his, hands that is, are like a toddler's game.
Palm to palm his fingertips tower over my own.
We try to never let him go hungry.

Two flower fae grace us tonight as well.
Not a matched pair by any means, but a perfectly
      balanced duet.

Traveling together when others go solo, and they too
    have strange tales to tell.
Each finishes the other's sentences, adding nuance and
    mirth.
They are a delight to watch.
I don't know them well, and I never do remember
    their names.
But who would not dream sweetly of them both?

Lastly there is the lady of the ravens.
She looks the most human of us all, though there is
    no debating her inclusion in our circle.
It is the fire that brings out her true nature.
The flickering shadows of dancing flames, showing
    feathers where before was simply silk.

She paints her memories in purples and blues,
    thinking they are only dreams.
While a sadness weighs heavy on her heart.
A kinship to old tortured souls, met before but long
    forgotten.

Her mind slips from time to time,
Like a record skipping back onto misplaced grooves
    momentarily.
A glimpse of hidden groves.
The truth of the world, that the world doesn't want.
So she retreats a little more.
One day she will break free of the strictures of society
    and slip below the hills with the rest of us.

Perhaps to linger there in happiness for a while.
To remember her wings.
But not tonight.

Me?

I'm just an old soul, freshly banished.
Wrapped in brown cloth, like a parcel wrapped in
    paper,and lost in the mail.
A little more torn and dirtied every day.
I just write what I see. And I say what I write.
Wicked and clever? Perhaps...
But the iron on my hip is not an act of aggression.
It is just a matter of self-defense.

I need not worry about such things here.
As I warm my feet at the fire, drying the striped socks
    I purchased from a wizard.
They are a common theme amongst our kind.
To set us apart from a sea of white ankles and tennis
    shoes.
As if the sparkle in our eyes, and the mischief in our
    smiles, did not already oblige.

We sing our songs, and we laugh at each other's lies.
We craft wondrous dreams, and hatch tantalizing
    schemes,
And we ponder how to saw a lady in half...
Without getting into trouble.

And any who stumble on us tonight might think we
    are an odd lot indeed;
A band of misfits and rogues.
If they only knew the half of it.

There is an offer of marshmallows, chocolate, and
    graham.
But feathers and fingers get sticky, with naught but
    leaves for napkins.
The ambassador ends up with melted mallow all over
    his shoes.

So we switch to gummy bears instead.
Skewered with a stick and held over the flames for just
    a moment, they become warm snotty jewels.
Like candy oysters, sucked down with relish and
    delight.
We don't speak of weighty matters.
We don't dwell on past losses, or the coming parting
    at the dawn.
We simply exist in the glow of each other's strange
    company.

And nothing happens...
Because nothing has to.

Author's Notes

"But a goblin is always something more than a mere monster. Goblins are reminders that something has been lost."

From the essay, "Grendel The Outsider" by Ari Berk, www.ariberk.com

It wasn't until after I had finished writing this book, and was well into page layout and formatting, that I stumbled upon this quote by my friend, and excellent author, Ari Berk. It struck me as incredibly profound and very appropriate to what had emerged as I gathered all of Gandersnitch's stories together. What started as merely three twisted faerie tales to entertain middle grade children, evolved into a journey of loss and the ever present hope of redemption.

Gandersnitch is a sort of monster. But he is also more. He is a bitter, womanizing, cad. Or as my wife puts it, a sexist bastard. She often, and loudly, has to remind herself that the character is not me. And I hope that the readers will understand that fact as well. He is, I think, a highly entertaining character, and to make him so, he is also intentionally terribly flawed. He is rooted in a Victorian mindset that reeks of chauvinism, cultural superiority, and at times, racism. (Though really, who doesn't hate Trolls?) When dealing with an adult audience, he can be offensive. And that is on purpose.

One of the many things I try to do with Gandersnitch is highlight the absurdities of human behavior through the comedy of an inhuman character. If you find yourself personally offended by his actions or words, I apologize; as that means I maybe was not as skillful with the joke as I had intended to be. Please, do not take this twisted goblin's ways as my endorsement of such behavior among actual people. As I have said many, many times, he is a terrible role model.

But ultimately, this book is about a journey. It is about a flawed absurdist character suffering the consequences of his own bad choices, rebuilding his life amid cascading setbacks, and looking towards the future with a dangerous grin, a quick and snarky wit, and an oversized pair of scissors.

Creating this book has been a journey for me as well. Throughout it I have learned many new things about writing, editing, design, and printing. I have made new friends in the self publishing world, and in those strangers who stepped in among my existing friends to help with the crowdfunding of the book. I have also discovered many new things about this character and the faint dangling threads of new tales to explore.

This journey of self publishing has been way more challenging than I expected and also infinitely more fulfilling than I could have imagined. There are two more books in progress with several others waiting in the wings. Neither of the next ones are about Gandersnitch, though there is the beginning of an extension of Otterbourne banging around in my mind that deals with—REDACTED—I was certainly not expecting that story to show up, but it did. I just have to take my time in telling it.

Lastly, I wish to confess that three of the poems in the book are not of my own composition. While it may be obvious to the readers, I would hate to take credit for other people's work, even when they are long dead.

"Little Bunny Foo Foo" is a traditional children's song that I often heard as a young child. Strangely enough, I do not believe that I have ever sung it to my own children.

"Barnacle Bill the Sailor" is a bawdy American drinking song first published in Immortalia (1927). There are many more lewd and lurid verses, and I truly hope some of my pirate-minded friends will pick this one up and start singing it at the Renaissance Faires I attend.

"Otterbourne" or "The Battle Otterbourne" is a traditional Scottish ballad catalogued by Francis James Child as Child Ballad #161. I have adapted the selected verses slightly, both to assist in their interpretation as a love song and so that the meter of the poetry will sound better to a modern American ear. I highly recommend that if you are not familiar with the Child Ballads, that you set aside an afternoon (or three) to peruse their treasures. I also suggest listening to the version of "Otterburn" sung by Tony Cuffe, which is amazingly beautiful, even if I cannot understand a single word he says.

I hope you have enjoyed these slices of Gandersnitch's journey. I hope in some sense, that it adds more magic to your life. For those of you expecting another poem in the book, I am sorry. It just did not fit in the end, but I will get it out there eventually.

In parting, I will steal yet another thing. Though Shakespeare is long dead, so I don't think he will mind if I abscond with the parting words of his most famous goblin, Puck.

If we shadows have offended,
Think but this, and all is mended—
That you have but slumbered here
While these visions did appear.
And this weak and idle theme,
No more yielding but a dream...

"That's right, it was all just a product of your own sick and twisted imagination. I am completely blameless! I did not force these fools to buy my book. I mean, seriously, what were they even thinking? I am a goblin! Hang around with me, and you are gonna get some filth on you... Sheesh."

—Robert (& Gandersnitch), November 2014

Aknowledgements

There are so many people to thank and so many who have contributed, in one way or another, to my own absurdity and imagination. The incredible creations of Brian Froud, Tony DiTerlizzi, Ari Berk, Gary Lippincott, Jim Henson, Charles de Lint, and Ian Lemke all helped influence the character that eventually became Gandersnitch the Goblin. I am also truly grateful for the support of my family, friends, and fans in making this book a reality.

First and foremost, a huge thank you to my amazing wife, Rebecca. It is she who designed and made all of Gandersnitch's costumes, provided the interior art for this book, makes more of the product we sell than anyone gives her credit for, transcribes my ramblings on cross country trips, helps me memorize my lines, and shows her support in so many uncountable ways. I could not have chosen a better partner with which to spend my life, and I am still in awe every day that she chose me as well.

To my father, for buying me my very first copy of D&D, and never hesitating to purchase another strange sci-fi or fantasy book on our frequent trips to the bookstore while on vacation with my sisters at his house.

To my mother, for taking me to my first drama classes and doing her best to always nurture my creativity. And to both of them for reading to us, especially the fairy tales.

To my own kids, Elowyn and John Dalton, for rolling their eyes when "Daddy is doing that crazy goblin voice again." For accepting that sometimes my only answer to their question can be a raised hand of "Please let me finish writing this sentence." For teaching me patience and pushing me to the understanding that being silly is actually a terribly important thing to do.

To Mab, for insisting that I write more stories and publish the damn book already. And for graciously lending her voice to the audiobook.

To Travis, for showing me that it was actually possible to publish a book on my own.

To Joshua, for being there at the beginning of Gandersnitch's creation, and well before, and for providing invaluable insight, suggestions, and encounters with strung out squirrels along the way.

To Duncan Eagleson, for being honest and professional in his critiques, and pushing me to dig deeper and keep polishing.

To the Smestads, for housing me each year and providing wonderful accommodations and company in which to write.

To Katie, for being my booth friend, confidant, and roommate and for encouraging me to share my poetry that first time at Faeriecon.

To the entirety of Strange Company, for welcoming me, accepting me, listening to me, laughing with and at me, and being an amazing sounding board for all sorts of insane ideas that will probably (and hopefully) never see the light of day. Please do not begrudge me the ones that I absconded with to include within these pages.

To Charles de Lint, not only for his amazing body of work that I discovered quite by accident among the hardbacks in a tiny used bookstore in Queens and read voraciously through my twenties, but more importantly for a comment in an elevator one night about needing to have my poetry published. That single moment gave me the confidence to finally transcribe my imagination down onto the page for others to read.

To the gremlins in my phone's GPS system that suddenly announced as I traveled down the highway at seventy miles an hour on the way to Spoutwood, "Turn right in 400 feet!" I knew they were wrong but I listened anyways, and thus discovered a winding road through a gorgeous state park of huge boulders and fallen trees. This incredible landscape prompted a poem, as most of my poetry begins while I drive. That poem, and a little glass mushroom I picked up at the Ohio Renaissance Faire while waiting on a man to engrave a new wedding band for my wife, became the seed that grew into the story "Otterbourne."

To Marc Hudgins, for taking my vague ideas and creating a truly awesome map. And for being a sounding board when I struggled over references to mythical inter-marriages.

To Billy Crocker and his musical partners in Ancien, for recording the title track of the audiobook and for entertaining me on many otherwise dull afternoons with their old world music at my booth.

To my beta readers: Dave, Travis, Steve, Kimberly, Kimberlie, both Michelles, Dana, James, Amy, Holly, Andrew, Katie, Stephanie, Samantha, Ray, Jenny, and Jeanne for pointing out errors in my early versions and suggesting alternative paths to explore. They were not always right, but they were always helpful.

And to my editor, Wendy, for enthusiastically working to cover up the fact that I never actually bothered to take Freshman English in college. Ok, that is a lie. I took it, but I only went to the first class.

To the generous people who supported this book financially and made it possible to have it printed, who are all listed in the manner in which they wished on the opposite page.

And lastly, to my departed grandfather, Lt. Colonel Eugene Dalton Cook, USAF. It his stories that taught me how to tell my own.

Thank you all.

A **SINCERE THANK YOU TO**: Travis Fessler of Pickled Brothers Circus; Her Majesty, Queen Ilex Aquifolia, Protector of Animals and Mistress of Wild Natural Places of the Maryland Faerie Festival; Aurra & Aleister Kendall; Mara & Spartakos Kendall; Mab Just Mab & Wedji Tucheeks; Merrilee Steele; Elle Mannion; The Russell Family; Thunder Jay Studio; Madison Metricula; Nastasya Ribakova; Amanda Bowen; Cassilynn L. Brown; Mellie from Fine Line Leather Design; Kimberlie Cruse; Barbara; Ursula Whiffenpott; Mike Cervantes; Bob & Tracy; Andy Cowen & the O'Rly Radio Podcast; The Sparkles; Joshua Leder; The Attic Shoppe Trading Company; Jeanne Wilkins; Esther Ellen Wildblood; Ray Ravenwolves, Stephanie Ravenwolves, Ashley Ravenwolves, & Stephen Ravenwolves; David Connell Olsher; Terry Racinskas & Barkley Snoot Fitzgerald; Lance Woolen; Jessica Gumtow (Pookagirlart); Pixie; Mary Layton; Leah and Mattew Volker; Angie Carter; Mindy, Joel & Erik; Jake Gotto; Ryan Spellman; Thomas & Olivia Davis; The Fairchild Family; George Stefanowich; Angela Hinton; Gryffan & Alexys; Peg Payne; Ian Lemke; Charles de Lint; Joshua Safford; Erin B. Dougherty; Michelle Yavitch Bucy; Jo King; Sean Baygents; Teus Kappen; The Dancing Dogs and Grinning Cats; Amy Fae January; Larry Wood - FantasyMasks.com; Jean Cartwright-Rosnick; Melissa "Trubble" Trotter; Edward von Hegner; Jonathan "Dr Archeville" Howell; Norah Hansen; Jeffry Rinkel; Banjo; Circle City Aerodrome; Kristina Reames; Tabbie >^..^<; The McGeary Family; Robert, Alexandra, & Ada Bush-Kaufer; Elizabeth Welke; Amy January; Emma Casale; Duncan Parke; Kimberly Stewart; Michael L. McMullen John & Emily Crumb; Glenn Herbert; Kim Fritts; Kelsey Stratton; Katie Lennon; Tonya Geer; Blue Flame Leather; Goblinheart; Sarah "ToadstoolsNTreestump" Dressler; Jack Kasliner; Dawn Przybylski; Jessica Welke & Jamie Schaeffer III; Rick Wales; Magus; Cecelia & Thor Thomas; and other anonymous donors for their support.

Robert A. Turk is a sculptor, mask maker, entertainer, author, poet, and slightly odd individual. He lives in a very old and possibly haunted house in Ohio, with his wonderful wife, his two incredibly creative children, an old lazy dog, and some rather uncolorful fish.